Copyright © 2024 by P.C. James and Kathryn Mykel All rights reserved.

No part of this book may be reproduced in any form or by any electronic or mechanical means, including information storage and retrieval systems, without written permission from the author, except for the use of brief quotations in a book review.

Copyright notice: All rights reserved under the International and Pan-American Copyright Conventions. No part of this book may be reproduced or transmitted in any form or by any means, electronic or mechanical, including photocopying and recording, or by any information storage and retrieval system, without permission in writing from publisher. This is a work of fiction. Names, places, characters, and incidents are either the product of the author's imagination or are used fictitiously, and any resemblance to any actual persons, living or dead, organizations, events, or locales is entirely coincidental. Warning: the unauthorized reproduction or distribution of this copyrighted work is illegal. Criminal copyright infringement, including infringement without monetary gain, is investigated by the FBI and is punishable by up to 5 years in prison and a fine of $250,000.

TABLE OF CONTENTS

1.	Whispers Among the Roses	1
2.	Guests, Gossip, and Garden Plans	9
3.	Grand Entrances and First Impressions	15
4.	The Garden Tour	24
5.	Lifeless in the Garden	29
6.	Unearthing Secrets	35
7.	Tea, Tidbits, and Tales	41
8.	Bones of Contention	50
9.	Unearthing the Truth	59
10.	A Rose By Another Name	66
11.	Petals of Perception	71
12.	Beneath the Surface	78
13.	Blooms and Alibis	93
14.	Snuff, Scandals, and Secrets	99
15.	The Scent of Trouble	105
16.	A Split Stem	110
17.	Chief Inspections	116
18.	A New Blossom	123
19.	Clearing the Weeds	130
20.	A Clue in Disguise	136
21.	The Snuff of Suspicion	146
22.	Blooms and Betrayals	160
23.	Thorns Beneath the Roses	169
24.	The Blooming Truth	177
25.	A Shift in the Garden	180
	About the Author P.C. James	185
	About the Author Kathryn Mykel	187

1

WHISPERS AMONG THE ROSES

Snodsbury Hall, England, June 1959

Lady Mary Culpeper, Duchess of Snodsbury, savored the sweet stillness of the summer afternoon, unaware that death's cruel hand would soon shatter the serene beauty of her estate.

The record player filled the air with a gentle tune. Though the end of the '50s had brought notable changes, it still resonated with its familiar, elegant rhythms. The azure sky, with its cotton-like clouds, stretched overhead as she sat in the terrace's shade, gazing out at her palatial estate. The air, redolent with the sweet fragrance of blooming flowers, wrapped around her like a silken shawl. *How swiftly the world has changed. Yet, how fortunate we are to have such a splendid day,* she mused, a contented smile playing on her lips. She eyed her plump corgi, Barkley, and his exuberant pursuit of the Holly Blue butterfly—an especially rare sighting during the June-gap of migration. His white and tan coat was plush and well-groomed once again. In the heart of the English countryside, life moved at a more measured pace. Tradition still held firm, though the whispers of modernity had crept into even the most aristocratic of circles.

She glanced at the glossy magazine resting beside her teacup of Earl Grey. *Vogue*, with its cover model donning a sleek Dior gown hinted that fashion, much like society, was evolving. Mary found comfort because some things—like the timeless grace of a well-tailored dress—never went out of style. The rose-patterned fabric she wore was a nod to the old guard, yet tailored with just enough finesse to keep her fashionable.

The steady hum of a motor car engine in the distance briefly interrupted her reverie. Since the war, the roads surrounding Snodsbury had seen more traffic, and sleek, chrome-trimmed automobiles.

A bead of sweat glistened on her forehead. She dabbed her face with her handkerchief, then slipped it back into the pocket of her sundress. She brushed a hand over her snowy hair, styled in loose waves which framed her face.

She stood to admire the polyantha roses, clustered in dense bunches, the garden bed by her side. She feathered her fingers against the velvety leaves as she strolled away from the house, down the terrace steps, and along the path.

Even her gardener, young Mr. Zaclan Tamberton, enjoyed the day—zipping about with a motorized wheelbarrow, a modern contraption well ahead of its time. Shocking to Mary at first, it proved undeniably efficient in maintaining her vast estate.

"Such is progress," she muttered softly to herself, watching Barkley trot lazily across the stone path, his short legs kicking up tiny clouds of dust.

The Royal Family had thrust the dog breed into the spotlight. Mary shared a deep connection with the young, corgi-loving Queen, who had tackled countless challenges since ascending to the throne in 1952—just as Mary had navigated the trials of widowhood and financial strain.

She scanned the lawn, stopping at Roland's memorial, sculpted to reflect the vigor of his youth. Everything was all so different from the day she'd returned to Snodsbury shortly after the war ended. Then, the house still bore the marks of every soldier billeted in its many rooms from when the government requisitioned the property in 1939. The government's compensation covered only a fraction of the estimate to repair all the damage. The estate bore witness to the soldiers' wartime training exercises and the sports necessary to keep them fit. Great concrete slabs used for 'heaven knows what' were everywhere throughout the grounds, and again the money to return the land wasn't close to the estimates for refurbishment. And the government's 'death duties' when Roland died meant there was only enough to keep Mary living quietly at the London house throughout the war and for a short time after.

Mary smiled. That was then. Now the Snodsbury estate, with its sprawling acres of greenery, once neglected, thrived under the careful tending of her new gardener. Her rejuvenated home mirrored her own revival. The duchess marveled at the riot of colors that surrounded her as she headed back up the path. Roses, blooming in every conceivable shade, created a breathtaking tapestry against the backdrop of the stately mansion. She circled back to the shade of the terrace and sat just out of reach of the sun's heat at the small table, in a straight-backed chair.

Ponsonby, her ever-dutiful butler, appeared at her side. Tall and impeccably dressed in a black tailcoat, his salt and pepper hair slicked back, he bore a silver tray with a delicate china teapot and matching cup. In a deep, resonant voice he announced, "Your tea," accompanied by a brief bow.

"Thank you, Ponsonby," Mary said, smiling, as he placed the

tray on the table and poured her a cup before handing her a dish with lemon wedges.

Mary placed one slice in her cup and waited for the flavor to blend into her tea.

Ah, the soothing embrace of warm tea, she thought, accepting the cup with a gracious nod. A sip revealed the aromatic blend, a harmony of flavors. "Thank you."

"And might I inform you, that preparations for the upcoming garden party are well underway." Ponsonby intoned, a subtle excitement in his voice.

Mary, her eyes shielded from the sun with a cupped hand, peered up at him. "Thank you, Ponsonby." Her mind flitted briefly to the approaching event, a chance to reaffirm her place among the aristocracy.

"RSVPs are flooding in. The guests are expecting a splendid affair," he continued, a neatly folded paper in hand.

"Fit for royalty." She chuckled, a playful echo of Cook's own words.

This occasion held more than the promise of a grand gathering; it was a triumph over financial woes, a testament to her resilience. *I've weathered storms and now I revel in the sunshine. All thanks to a royal dispatch from the Queen.* Guiding the final cohort of debutantes through their meticulous training the previous year not only marked a significant responsibility but also emerged as the key to resolving Mary's financial predicament, ushering in a flush of prosperity once more. The weight of this newfound responsibility added a layer of importance to the upcoming party, intertwining Mary's personal triumphs with the flourishing beauty of her restored estate.

"Excellent, Ponsonby. I do hope the weather holds," she mused, looking toward the sky.

"As do we all," Ponsonby concurred. "The new arbor has

garnered much admiration. Its intricate lattice design complements the garden splendidly."

Her favorite feature was the elegant chandelier. She'd paid extra to have the wiring extended from the house, and the way the crystals scattered soft rainbows—especially on the evenings they used outdoor table settings—was money well spent.

"Agreed. Mr. Tamberton has outdone himself and exceeded all of my expectations." Mary's gaze shifted to the recently erected arbor at the heart of the garden. The intertwining vines and climbing roses were already scaling its structure, creating a romantic canopy beneath. The babbling fountain, another addition to the evolving landscape, whispered a comforting melody. *A balm for my heart that still longs for Roland.* "I must express my gratitude to Zaclan for transforming these gardens into a paradise."

"Indeed, Mr. Tamberton takes great pride in his work," Ponsonby replied.

Barkley, with his short legs and roly-poly girth, bounded up the terrace steps, tail wagging in blissful abandon. He lapped water from his bowl and then settled under her wrought-iron chair. Mary leaned back, closing her eyes for a moment. *This day holds an air of serenity.*

With a theatrical entrance, Cook pushed through the patio doors. "Milady, excuse my interruption," she announced. Mary opened her eyes and turned her gaze to her cook as the employee sashayed her rotund figure toward Mary and Ponsonby. Cook's expressive gestures demanded attention. "But we must go over the final menu to ensure everything can be properly consumed while standing." The stout woman in traditional white jacket, apron, and ruched cap, handed Mary the written menu:

- Delicate Finger Sandwiches—elegant bites of cucumber and cream cheese, as well as smoked salmon with lemon and dill—the crusts neatly trimmed.
- Scones—tender, flaky pastries, served with generous dollops of clotted cream and strawberry jam.
- Pork Pies—hearty, hand-sized pastries, filled with seasoned minced pork and encased in a crispy crust.
- Coronation Chicken Salad—a dish created for the coronation of the Queen herself—a flavorful concoction of diced chicken, mixed with curry-flavored mayonnaise, dried fruit, and almonds, served atop slices of toast.

"Of course, we'll also serve the customary pastries and cakes, such as Victoria sponge, and for beverages: fresh lemonade and various teas. It'll be a symphony of culinary delights that would tantalize the taste buds of even the aristocracy."

"I have no doubts in your ability to carry out the task," Mary assured while she nodded.

Cook beamed, her pudgy flour-dusted cheeks turning crimson, then she curtsied and took her leave.

"Shall we go over the RSVPs, Your Grace?" Ponsonby asked.

Mary stirred her drink absentmindedly as Ponsonby read out the list, her mind far from the upcoming garden party. Despite the idyllic scene of her flourishing estate, a dark cloud hovered over her thoughts.

"Please, continue. Tell me Eleanor is going to be here?"

"Yes. Also, Lord and Lady Abernoothy, and the Duchess of Mothford." The rest of the names echoed through the air as Ponsonby announced the invited guests. In any other year, this event would be a mere social formality, an opportunity to uphold her family's legacy. Yet, this time, it carried a weight far greater than simple pleasantries and polite conversation.

This party was not just about displaying her restored estate. It was a vital chance to cement her financial recovery and maintain her precarious standing in Society.

"Also, Sir Jolyon Steele—"

Mary quirked a single brow. "Is he still dabbling in the snuff business?"

She had fought her way back from near ruin—her title alone wasn't enough to shield her from whispers of misfortune. The last thing she needed was another scandal, and there were rumors about the select group of men still enamored of this now-frowned-upon tobacco habit.

Ponsonby nodded with a hint of reservation. "Yes, I believe so."

"Well, that should be interesting. Though we must steer clear of any catastrophe," Mary remarked.

He frowned, but quickly composed his best butler's expression. "Hopefully, just a little spice," he replied with a hint of mischief in his tone. "But not too much, Your Grace."

Mary chuckled at the lapse in his decorum and quick turnaround to his mild-mannered concern.

"Ponsonby, the guest list sounds impeccable," she said, her tone light though her mind was far from at ease.

Her concern was simple. In the years leading up to the war, and Roland's death, she'd been one of the most prominent members of England's social world. And her exploits, with fellow amateur sleuths, had made her famous even beyond that. They'd solved many serious crimes leading to the arrest and imprisonment of murderers and more. Then, during the war, she'd worked hard organizing medical services for wounded servicemen and bombed-out families; she'd been recognized by a grateful Crown and government for that work.

Roland's death began the slow slide into comparative poverty and finally anonymity as she'd found she no longer could face the well-wishers and their endless condolences. New people and faces filled the upper ranks of the social world, and she was forgotten, it seemed. Friends and acquaintances faded away. Death and their own fall from wealth took many of them. Emigration took many others because England wasn't recovering from the war the way so many other countries were. Then that letter came from the Palace, and she seemed to awaken from a dark, dreamless sleep as she prepared the debutantes for what turned out to be the last debutante ball that had the favor of the Palace. Solving the murder of the woman who was to have prepared the debs had been the icing on the cake.

Who in the Palace had remembered her? Eleanor said she'd proposed that Mary take on the role because Eleanor's mother had been one of Mary's fellow sleuths in the '30s, but the decision had been made at the top. The Queen herself had decreed it so, though she could hardly have remembered Mary or Roland. Mary sighed. It didn't matter now, why the Queen had chosen her. She, Mary, would not let her down.

She would demonstrate that the trust had not been misplaced, even in such simple things as once again leading the county of Norfolk in a respectable social life. This first garden party, and there would be future events for all walks of life in Norfolk, would lead to a return to normality. *Nothing can go wrong.*

2

GUESTS, GOSSIP, AND GARDEN PLANS

Awaiting her young sleuths' arrival, Mary admired the finished garden from the terrace. A voice interrupted her solitude. "Good morning, neighbor," Quiggly Smythe said as he popped his head around a large hedge, his round face bright red and beaming with curiosity. She sighed. Since the day she and Roland arrived at the Snodsbury estate, he had been a 'local color' she wanted to do without.

At her side, Barkley sneezed, but didn't waver from his post.

"Good morning, Mr. Smythe," Mary replied with a polite smile, albeit not a welcoming one. She had purposefully omitted inviting him to the party, yet somehow, here he was—convenient timing.

"I've been watching the splendid transformation of your garden from my property across the field," Quiggly exclaimed, stepping into full view. "And that Mr. Tamberton is quite the artist with plants, isn't he?"

Mary nodded. "Yes, Mr. Tamberton has truly worked wonders. The garden party is approaching, and I'm delighted with the way everything is coming together."

Quiggly continued to chatter about the garden's progress,

and Mary behaved politely to the tedious man, but it was a pleasant surprise when Ponsonby, with his customary decorum, announced the arrival of the trio. "My lady, the young ladies have just arrived."

Thank goodness, the girls have arrived just in time. I am so delighted to see them and to get to enjoy their youthful spirit again.

Barkley fidgeted, then he sniffed imperiously at Mr. Smythe's ankles. "Easy." Mary put her hand down by her side with an open palm, halting his movements. *I might not be able to contain him once he knows the girls are here, but for now at least, he must maintain the decorum his royal pedigree demands.* Barkley, a distant relative of the Queen's own corgis, obeyed commands and always understood exactly what others expected of him.

"My guests are arriving, Mr. Smythe," Mary said. "I must meet them. Goodbye."

Ponsonby escorted Smythe away, as he'd done time and time again—around the side of the building and toward his own property.

A polished car pulled up the driveway, dusting off the gravel as it came to a halt. Winnie, Dotty, and Margie, all poking their heads out of the window, looking fresh-faced and enthusiastic, emerged from the vehicle with a flourish most unladylike. Mary's heart warmed to see them again, and she and Barkley both let decorum fly out the window, like the girls' hair.

"Ah, my dear girls! Welcome to Snodsbury." She greeted them with open arms. Barkley, bounded toward them enthusiastically.

After exchanging pleasantries, the group made their way inside. The grand entrance hall, adorned with marble columns and an elaborate chandelier, welcomed them with an air of aristocratic splendor.

The girls, chattering excitedly, recounted the tales of their days since they'd last seen Lady Mary.

"As I understand it, neither Dotty's nor Margie's parents will be in attendance this time." Mary's gaze momentarily flickering toward the two aforementioned young girls who didn't appear to be disappointed. "But your parents will be here tomorrow, Winnie?"

"Yes, they'll be here." Winnie stood tall, her perfect posture giving her an air of authority that belied her nineteen years.

While the girls played with Barkley, bringing out giggles all around, they finally settled into the elegant sitting room, where the conversation shifted to the colorful characters who would grace the garden party.

Mary filled them in. "The notable guests expected tomorrow are a blend of aristocracy, eccentricity, and refined taste. Many of them you will know, of course, but only as your parents' friends or acquaintances, I fear. I'll tell you a little more so you will know what to talk to them about. Lord and Lady Abernoothy, are renowned for their philanthropy and passion for the arts. They will regale you with tales of their travels, art collection, and the various charitable causes they support. It may be tedious to you younger folk, but please try to look interested."

Dotty giggled at Mary's description and request for understanding of their elders' peccadilloes. Barkley helped the mood by prancing around the three girls, all sitting on a long sofa. He elicited more smiles and gentle pats now that everyone had settled. He occasionally sniffed around the room.

Mary continued, "The Duchess of Mothford is very witty, with a sharp intellect. She has a penchant for engaging in lively conversations on politics. She may even grace us with a captivating reading of a piece of classical poetry."

Winnie groaned and rolled her eyes. "I'll avoid her then." Margie and Dotty said nothing, but their expressions suggested they agreed with Winnie.

Barkley found a cozy spot by Mary's side. With a contented

sigh, he curled up, his watchful eyes still peering around the room.

Amid the conversation, Cook entered the sitting room with a silver tray. She balanced a teapot and set of teacups, accompanied by a selection of biscuits. With a warm smile, she distributed the refreshments to the guests.

"Cook, now that we have maids in employment again, you no longer need to concern yourself with serving the tea."

"Yes, milady, but I'm part of the six, here with you!" With a twitch of her lips, she half-bowed and exited.

"And, of course, Winnie's parents, Edward and Patricia Winters. Maybe you could tell us about them, Winnie? What do they like, for instance?"

Winnie stood, in her tailored shirt and high-waisted indigo skirt, and spoke confidently. "Thank you. Let me, Lady Mary."

Mary nodded, and Winnie poured the tea.

"My parents, Edward and Trish, have a keen interest in tradition, aristocracy, and familial customs—especially gatherings like this and the holidays," she stated, as if reading from a telegram. "And Mum can't sleep, which makes her grumpy, and Dad never stops worrying about me—yes, they are as boring as all that suggests."

Margie laughed, and Dotty added, "Aren't all old people boring?"

"You won't think so one day. And, despite Winnie's naughty remarks, I'll be pleased to make their acquaintance again." Mary sipped from her cup as warm steam rose, bringing the aromatics to her nose. "Then we have Sir Jolyon Steele, a gentleman with an eccentric edge, who will be instantly recognizable by his bold fashion choices. Despite his peculiarities, he's been a beloved fixture in high society since I was a girl. He is an aficionado of snuff, or so I'm told."

Margie, unable to contain a mischievous grin, joked, "The 'Snufarati' are coming, it seems!"

The three girls burst into laughter, biscuit crumbs flying everywhere, and Barkley jumped into action, cleaning up the unexpected treat.

Frowning at the girls, and the dog, Mary also rebuked a vision of a clandestine society of snuff enthusiasts—nicknamed the Snufarati—converging on her estate. *Oh, heavens no!*

Ponsonby, with a keen ear to the conversations of the afternoon, approached. "Ah, Miss Margery, you might find this amusing to learn that Sir Jolyon is, in fact, a member of SNUF: the Society of the New United Fellows. They take great pride in their appreciation for snuff and other finer things in life."

Dotty flashed a puzzled expression, her ginger-colored brows drawn into the center. "What is snuff exactly?"

"Snuff is a finely ground tobacco, often inhaled through the nose. It was quite popular in the past, especially among the upper classes. People used to take snuff as enjoyment, much like smoking—"

Interrupting Mary's explanation, the young, attractive gardener—a titled gentleman whose family, like Mary, had fallen on hard times—strolled into view, causing a stir among her listeners. Adorned in a well-fitted shirt with rolled-up sleeves, he carried a basket of freshly cut flowers.

As the trio of amateur sleuths' eyes widened in collective fascination, Mary seized the moment to take the girls outside and make introductions, realizing that the dashing figure indeed captivated the young ladies as they approached.

"Ladies, allow me to present Zaclan Tamberton, our esteemed gardener and the creative mind behind the magnificent transformation of our gardens. Mr. Tamberton, these are the talented young ladies I was telling you about—Winnefred Winters, Dorothy Dillyard, and Margery Marmalade."

The distinguished gardener, with a slight bow and a warm smile, acknowledged the introduction. "A pleasure to make your acquaintance, ladies. Call me Zac, all my friends do."

Twirling her skirt back and forth, Margie squealed most unladylike before quickly composing herself. "You may call us: Winnie, Dotty, and Margie."

"I've heard much about your enthusiasm for mysteries and adventures," Zac continued.

The trio, enchanted and a bit flustered, exchanged quick glances and managed polite curtsies. Winnie, the least affected by his charms, her sleek, black hair parted and her nails meticulously trimmed, extended a hand. "The pleasure is ours, Mr. Tamberton."

He shot out a dirt-stained hand that Winnie politely shook. "We've been eager to explore the wonders of the new gardens, and, of course, assist Lady Mary in any way we can."

Zac's gaze lingered on each of the ladies as he shook their hands. "I'm delighted to have such charming company."

As Ponsonby emerged again, the girls straightened and reined in their enthusiasm.

Mary flashed him a grateful look. *Thank goodness these girls are of age, otherwise I'd have my hands full trying to keep them away from Mr. Tamberton. As it is, any one of them would be a good match for the jaunty young man.*

"May I?" The gardener crooked his elbow toward Dotty, who squealed under her breath—blushing pink under her freckles—and accepted the proffered arm. "Shall we all go out and explore the garden and the maze?"

"Maze?" the girls echoed.

3

GRAND ENTRANCES AND FIRST IMPRESSIONS

The day of the garden party began inauspiciously with light summer rain in the morning, wetting the lawns and leaving puddles on the garden paths. By noon, however, after fervent wishing, hoping, and prayers by Mary, Ponsonby, and the three young sleuths, the sun made its appearance, and everything was drying up beautifully.

Soon the Snodsbury estate car was ferrying guests that arrived by train, to the house. The driveway was a constant stream of large cars belonging to the guests who lived close enough to be driven over in their own vehicles. Mary was weary of greeting guests by the time the river of bodies subsided, and she hurried to the terrace to see how Ponsonby and the maids were coping. Her butler and staff moved through the crowd, offering drinks and small dainties to the dozens of guests.

When she'd stood at the door welcoming the guests, her heart had been racing, doubt gnawing at her mind whether they'd hired enough staff for the event. But as her gaze darted around, everyone was in action, moving with purpose and efficiency, so she knew Ponsonby had judged it right. Watching the team scurrying around, attending to every detail, Mary felt a surge of pride. They were a well-oiled machine, a testament to their meticulous planning. No one waited impatiently, and everything seemed to flow seamlessly. A small smile tugged at the corners of Mary's lips as she realized her fears had been unfounded.

Seeing Lord and Lady Abernoothy engaged in an animated conversation with Eleanor, Mary crossed the terrace to join them.

"I'm so glad you could all come," she said, greeting them. "The weather has turned out gloriously for us." The weather was always a useful conversation starter in a country where it changed by the minute.

"Quite, quite," Lord Abernoothy said. "Mary, where's young Tamberton hiding? I have some snuff news for him. Don't tell me you've banished him below the stairs just because of the garden remodeling."

Mary laughed. "I'm sure Zaclan will be here soon. He's likely making himself handsome for the girls. They've all promised to be on the garden tour he's leading, and you know how young people are."

The group laughed politely. "Eleanor and I were just saying how much we're looking forward to the tour," Lady Abernoothy said. "My Lord and I have known young Zac since he was a baby —he was such a beautiful boy—and Eleanor has yet to meet him. We're as anxious as my dear husband is to see him." She tittered, and cast a sideways glance at her husband who sighed, no doubt used to his wife's teasing.

Lord Abernoothy was an older man, gray-haired, but still upright in his posture, a fine figure of a man, a novelist might say. His wife was a younger, pretty woman, only forty in age but sporting the fashions of a much younger woman. 'Mutton dressed as lamb' the more unkind members of society gossiped, when Lady Abernoothy wasn't there.

Eleanor was as refreshing as Mary remembered. An attractive young woman who seemed older than her years. No doubt because of living life by palace protocol—the job suiting her serious personality.

"Ah," Mary exclaimed. "Here's the man of the hour."

The others followed her gaze to the door where Zac Tamberton was coolly watching, waiting for the moment to join the throng. A handsome young man with his chin held as high as his confidence. Catching Mary's eye, he nodded and then crossed the terrace to join her.

Barkley yawned from his position by her side.

Mary tsked. *Are we keeping you awake, my pup?*

"About time too," Lord Abernoothy said jovially, as Tamberton arrived beside them. "I was just telling Mary, I wanted to see you."

"Good afternoon, Abernoothy," Zac said, smiling and taking a glass of white wine from the tray of a passing server. "And my lady," he added, smiling broadly at Lady Abernoothy.

Lady Abernoothy's smile had something about it that rather disturbed Mary, but she dismissed it. "Don't let his lordship monopolize you, Zaclan." Mary smiled and tapped her wrist, naked of a fancy watch. "You have a tour to guide in only ten minutes."

Abernoothy sipped his gin. "Monopolize, I won't. I only want to ask this young fellow about the snuff he gave me to try at our last society meeting, and where he got it. Damn fine product, you know."

Tamberton laughed. "A recipe of my own," he said. Then leaning toward Mary he spoke quietly, "When I'm not designing gardens for country estates, I dabble in creating unique snuffs."

"You don't say," Abernoothy replied in a dry tone. "And, Mary, he's a dab hand at that too. That's what I wanted to say. I'll take another ounce, if you've one to spare. You should give the society members a tour of your snuff production, my boy."

"If the members would welcome a youngster like me showing off." Tamberton chuckled. "I would be happy to do just that. As for another ounce, I'll give you half an ounce before you leave this weekend and the balance at the next meeting."

"Enough about that vile stuff," Lady Abernoothy cried. "I can't understand what you men find so fascinating about it."

"Here, here," Mary agreed. "Like everything tobacco related, it's horrible for your health."

Abernoothy and Tamberton exchanged glances. Tamberton then angled toward Eleanor and said, "Two on each side. Will you weigh in and break the tie? Tell me the Palace agrees with the gentlemen."

"I can't speak for the Palace on this matter, Mr. Tamberton," Eleanor said, and nodded to Mary. "But I side with the ladies."

Barkley barked, causing Mary to laugh. "Seems the dog is with us as well."

Tamberton opened his mouth but quickly closed it when Margie, Winnie, and Dotty joined them. He grinned instead. "Welcome, ladies. I hope you haven't come just to gang up on us poor men as well."

Margie's brow shot up. "What about?"

"Snuff," Tamberton replied in a jovial tone.

Dotty grimaced and stuck her tongue out. "Yuck!"

"Sniffing, snuffling, and sneezing." Winnie wrinkled her nose, interrupting her refined, statuesque features. "I'm with whoever here was against it."

"We were," Mary said, chuckling. "It's a pleasure to find we all concur." She glowered at the two men, adding, "Horrible habit."

"Is snuff worse than a pipe?" Margie asked, her wide eyes reflecting genuine curiosity.

Lady Abernoothy glared at her husband and answered Margie's question, "Definitely."

"Perhaps we should leave the ladies to enjoy their cocktails, and we'll get that half ounce now," Lord Abernoothy suggested to Tamberton.

"Oh no, you don't," Winnie cried, the cool undertones of her pale complexion flushing. "We're here for the tour that starts in" —She glanced at the modest wristwatch she wore—"three minutes."

The men voiced their own dissent, and Tamberton hooted. Holding up his hand, he conceded, "I'm convinced." He drew a small metal pointer from his pocket and *ting-ting*-ed on his glass. When he had the crowd's attention, he said, loud enough to be heard along the entire terrace, "The garden tour will begin in two minutes. Please gather at the fountain, where we shall start."

He turned back to Mary and the others, saying, "Follow me, ladies, if you're taking the tour. And Lord Abernoothy, I'll fetch you that half ounce when I'm back from the tour."

Leading the small group down the steps to the lawn, the gardener meandered his way to the ornate fountain—made up of dolphins and plump cherubs—that stood at the start of the formal gardens, edged with low box hedges.

Mary hadn't gone far when she felt her ankle brushed by the furry body of her plump corgi. "Barkley," she exclaimed. "You'll trip me up, surprising me like that."

Barkley took no notice and trotted forward to join Tamberton and the girls.

Mary caught Ponsonby shooting her a pointed look. She excused herself to the Abernoothys, "I'll just be a moment." Then she hurried away.

At the edge of the terrace, Ponsonby greeted Mary, though he kept a watchful eye on the temporary staff. "Your Grace."

She held back a grin. Mary always knew she was in *disgrace* when Ponsonby grew formal with her title.

"Yes?" She asked, her voice light and full of playful energy as she leaned in.

"Many of your guests are not going on the tour," he reminded her.

"I have to go, Ponsonby, to see there's no funny business with the girls. I leave my remaining guests in your capable hands."

Mary considered which of her old friends from years past she wanted him to mingle with when Ponsonby stated, "I think Mr. Smythe is back, skulking in the shrubbery, my lady." He nodded toward the hedge maze.

Mary swept her eyes over the clumps of bushes but didn't see anyone. "Are you sure?"

Ponsonby nodded again. "He keeps out of sight most of the time, but once the tour begins, he'll have no choice but to move or risk being spotted."

"You're sure it's him?" Mary asked.

"He stays well hidden, my lady, but who else would it be?" Ponsonby replied.

"Bother! That man!" Mary huffed. "Completely impossible to snub."

A normal person would've realized that not getting an invitation by mail and then again getting omitted from a verbal invitation today, meant his presence wasn't required. *I simply don't want him at my party.*

"He doesn't take hints, my lady," Ponsonby replied as his blue eyes darkened and his brow furrowed. "Shall I have some of the male staff toss him out?"

I really shouldn't think it was a hint. Mary pursed her lips. *I'd like to do that, but it would cause questions and potentially spoil the afternoon.* She shook her head. "No. We'll let him lurk and pretend to be a guest, if that's what he wants."

"Very well, my lady," Ponsonby said. "However, I suspect it might lead to unpleasantness before the day is out."

"I'll rely on you to nip anything like that in the bud," Mary replied. "Now, I shall mingle, and you, my dear friend, shall watch what my nosey neighbor does." She saw her and Roland's old friend Sir Jolyon, trying to catch her eye from a small knot of elderly men, and she crossed the terrace to join them.

"Hello, my dear," Sir Jolyon said, taking Mary's hand in his own. "These fellows are members of the SNUF Society and want to know when young Tamberton will be available to join us?" The men protested at this blunt question, making Mary laugh.

"If it was any other gardener, Sir Jolyon," Mary replied, "I'd say only twenty minutes, but Zaclan is a fanatic about soils, fertilizer, plants, and Capability Brown—the greatest landscape artist ever. I fear the ladies who I see setting out with him may be a while."

"We don't care how long the ladies are, Lady Mary," Horace Higgenbottom, one of the older of the group, and a famous dandy in his day, declared. "So long as young Tamberton is back in time to explain his most recent snuff recipe."

A bewhiskered and stately man, once a diplomat, echoed Sir Jolyon's complaint. "He was very secretive about it when he spoke at the last society meeting." A general rumble of agreement followed this.

"Well, gentlemen," Mary replied, chuckling, "Zaclan has the choice between you fine elderly fellows and a bevy of beautiful young women hanging on his every word. I'm sure I know his choice."

"Put like that," Sir Jolyon guffawed. "I think I have time for another drink." He waved to a nearby server, and once she arrived the group exchanged their empty glasses for fresh ones.

Mary waited for their returned attention. "Has snuff come back into fashion? I hadn't heard such news."

"For some, yes. And for a select few," Donald Kelvinstone, an elderly man given to theatrical expressions, said dramatically, waving his glass around, "it's never been out of fashion. I hope it never becomes fashionable in the wider world again. Cheapens the product." He shuddered with the same exuberance.

"But it's a great inconvenience to us all, Donald," George Patron exclaimed. "Unless more of the wider world takes part, we shall never be able to partake of our delicious addiction in polite society. We need other people to join in."

"Pooh," Donald retorted, waving his exquisitely manicured hands at them. "We set the tone that others will follow. Producing scented snuff for those without an appreciation of the art, devalues it. I shall fight such, to the end." He finished with a grand flourish.

The others laughed. They were clearly used to Donald's poses.

"In case you hadn't guessed, Mary," Sir Jolyon interjected. "Zac is the philistine producing various scented snuffs that Donald objects to. We mere mortals think having some new variety can only bring snuff back into wider use. And anything is better than those awful cigarettes the common man smokes nowadays."

"I say 'a plague on all your houses,'" Mary replied, laughing, "for snuff *and* cigarettes. Now a pipe or cigar, those are the things for gentlemen."

A chorus of protest erupted from those assembled, showing that they did not share her view. "Peace!" she cried, laughing even harder. "I will send Zaclan to you the moment he returns from the garden tour with the ladies. Now, I must go. I fear they've been waiting too long for me."

She hurried across the terrace, only to be caught by Winnie's parents, Edward and Trish.

"You didn't want to join Winnie on the garden tour?" Mary asked.

"We've already missed it, surely," Winnie's mother replied. "We've been so entertained in a conversation with your neighbors, the Youngs."

"Let's hurry over. They'll likely be awaiting my return," Mary suggested.

"Oh good. I was hoping to sneak a few tips from your gardener. Ours is an elderly man who cuts the grass and only occasionally weeds the flower beds. I'd like to create something for the garden that future generations can enjoy."

"Then Mr. Tamberton is your man," Mary agreed, laughing as Ponsonby approached.

"Yes?" Mary asked, stepping away from her guests just enough to be out of earshot. "What is it, Ponsonby?"

"Our intruder is still in the shrubs, and, as I thought, has moved, so he isn't visible by the tour, but I'm worried about his intentions, my lady. I think we must do more than just watch him."

"You think he's lying in wait to attack the tour?" Mary asked, puzzled.

"Who can say what such a person might do, my lady, but whatever he's waiting to do can't be good for your guests or your day."

"Whatever he might be when in London with thugs at his beck and call, Ponsonby, here he's just a pathetic little creature. Zac will have no trouble dealing with him if he really is intending harm."

4

THE GARDEN TOUR

Mary trailed along behind Winnie's parents, the Winters, and nodded to Zac to proceed. Dotty fidgeted with the hem of her sleeve as the group waited for the older guests to join them at the fountain, and the three girls jostled close to Tamberton.

Of the twenty people joining the tour, there were only four men. Mary chuckled as she watched the three young sleuths close ranks on Zac like guards.

He began by introducing himself, speaking animatedly of his fascination from an early age with the great landscape artists of the past. Next he outlined the ideas behind his garden design and what they should see as they traveled from point to point. He wrapped up his informal speech by asking the group if they had questions.

Clasping their hands in a prayer, the three girls all frowned when one man asked about the history of landscape gardening in England. Fortunately, Zac dealt with the topic quickly, and they were soon setting out to the first vantage point.

The girls hung on Tamberton's every word, clearly more interested in the gardener himself than the actual content of his prose. For the rest of the participants, however, every plant was to be discussed in great detail—what soil, what shade, what watering, what attention each needed, what hardiness it exhibited—and every stop led to more questions. It seemed each person had their own ideas about every single plant.

Ambling through the maze, with its high hedges, was hot, as the sun warmed the heavy air, without a breeze to penetrate the maze's hedged walls. Suddenly, Zac led them into the open lawn at the center, and the air was fresh again. An icy blast of water sent the girls shrieking around like squawking chickens and Zac waving his hands to block the drenching. He ran to the sprinkler and twisted the nozzle to spray in the opposite direction.

Zac rejoined the three girls, drenched, his white shirt clinging to his lean, muscular frame. They stared at one another momentarily, then burst out laughing.

"This tour is turning out to be more interesting than I thought it would be," Lady Abernoothy whispered to her husband, loud enough for Mary to hear.

"Calm down, dear," he replied, grinning. "This is a public place."

"Ladies, gentlemen," Zac called out to the giggling group as he pulled the sodden shirt away from his skin to make it a little less revealing, "it may be best if I, and these three young ladies, leave to change. Can we reconvene at the fountain in thirty minutes?"

"Don't go together," Mary warned.

The three young ladies peered at each other as if only just realizing their blouses were similarly transparent. Mary's warning was regarding that what had been mildly exciting in Zac's case was a lot more than that in theirs.

"We can't turn around until they're all gone," Dotty whispered to her friends.

The touring party, however, seemed unwilling to stop the

tour, with much quiet argumentation among themselves about what to do under the circumstances.

Zac joined the three sleuths. "We could keep going, with us in the lead, until our clothes dry."

"I'm cold," Margie said, shivering.

"Now that we're out of the maze, the sun will soon dry and warm us," Winnie said, arms crossed, radiating a quiet control. "I agree with Dotty and Zaclan. We keep facing forward and continue with the crowd behind us."

The young gardener relayed this solution to the tour group, who quickly accepted it. "I'll lead us quickly from the shade, cast by the maze, and into the sunshine," Zac said to the crowd. "Don't want my three fellow victims to catch pneumonia."

Even as they made their way into the sun, the tour party was still whispering.

"Whatever Zac says," Dotty whispered. "I'm continuing straight on. My blouse is still completely see-through."

"At least we're decent though," Winnie pronounced. "It's no different to a swimsuit."

Dotty snorted. "I wouldn't be wandering around anyone's garden in my swimsuit, not even Lady Mary's."

Winnie chortled.

"You're hopeless, Dotty," Margie said through a laugh. "No one cares about that sort of thing nowadays."

"I care," Dotty cried, "and that's what's important."

The next stop on the tour was the rose garden, newly restored to its Victorian splendor under the bright sun. Zac told the tour how his research had led him to find early photographs of the rose garden, as well as watercolor paintings by the young daughters of the household from the late 1800s. Using these as his inspiration, he'd revived the garden with a modern twist.

Zac spoke more quickly now, with a slight shiver, no doubt

Royally Snuffed

on purpose for dramatic effect so he could get back to the house and change into dry clothes.

"You didn't mention how deep the beds are," an elderly woman asked. "Or what soil preparation you used."

He forced a smile. "I didn't need to dig deep beds," Zac continued, without skipping a beat. "The soil lacked compaction. In some areas, it was surprisingly loose. And that old standby, horse manure is best for roses. Fortunately, there are lots of horses in this neighborhood." He winked, piling on a now-fading charm.

Laughter rippled through the group, and Zac headed the tour back toward the house, still describing the gardens as they walked. "I'm sorry to cut the tour short, we must go change after all, but I encourage you all to take some time later this afternoon to make your own way around the gardens, seeing them from different locations. It'll be well worth your time and energy, I promise."

The tour participants dispersed, allowing Mary and the Winters to follow the three sleuths and Zac, who were running into the house to change. As they went, Winnie asked, "Where shall we meet back, and when?"

Dotty and Margie proposed a time and place, quickly arranging a rendezvous spot before they even reached the top of the stairs.

"What about you, Zac?" Dotty asked. "Will you be joining us?"

"Maybe later," he called back to them as he set off up the second flight of stairs to his room on the upper floor. "After I've changed, there's something I need to do first."

Margie muttered to her two friends, "What's he up to?"

Dotty shrugged. "Probably that snuff business."

"Maybe he wants to know who set that sprinkler on," Winnie replied with a steady gaze, "and give them a piece of his mind."

"Wait, Zaclan," Lord Abernoothy called, seeing the young man racing up the stairs. "I'll be there in a minute for my half ounce." He set off in pursuit of Zac.

Mary set her eyes on Winnie's parents. "What a thing to happen. Now, while they change, and Abernoothy gets his promised snuff from Zac, we should return to the terrace and join the other guests."

Winnie's father, who'd been watching his daughter anxiously, nodded. "Yes. There's no harm done. An automatic sprinkler, is it?"

"You must ask Mr. Tamberton when he comes down, Edward," Mary replied. "I'm afraid I only pay the gardening bills. He handles the fine details."

"He mentioned extending the rose garden even farther," Winnie's mother said to Mary. "Is that going to be this year?"

"I believe so," Mary replied, her thoughts already racing, wondering how to deal with the witty, sarcastic remarks she knew the other guests would unleash when she rejoined them. The drenching incident was too ripe a target for the amateur comedians among them to resist.

Mr. and Mrs. Winters exchanged a silent glance between them. Something unspoken in their eyes stirred unease in Mary. *Is that concern for their daughter in my care—a father's quiet worry over propriety?*

5

LIFELESS IN THE GARDEN

Mary glanced around the vibrant gardens, the scent of roses mingling with the laughter and chatter of her guests. The party was at its peak, and she reveled in the joyous atmosphere. But Barkley's howling disrupted the merriment, drawing her attention away.

"What's got into you, Barkley?" Mary murmured, squinting at the dog's frantic movements. He darted around, urging her to follow and then ran toward the rose garden.

Confused, Mary followed the corgi, his barks echoing through the air and her heart racing with apprehension. At the edge of the lawn, she caught Ponsonby's eye, and he nodded. She rushed behind the now yelping dog and through the gardens to a secluded corner, with Ponsonby's footfalls not far behind them. Barkley stopped abruptly on his haunches. The pup fixed his gaze on something amid the blossoms.

Mary froze, her breath hitching in her throat as her eyes fell on the lifeless figure of the talented gardener, Zaclan Tamberton, sprawled among the rose bushes. She took an unsteady step forward, the world narrowing in on the sight in front of her. The once vibrant young man lay face down in the horse manure spread generously among the rosebushes. The roses themselves, vivid and alive, now a cruel contrast to the chilling scene.

"Oh, dear!" Mary gasped, her hand flying to her mouth in disbelief as she recoiled instinctively.

At that moment, time stood still. Her heart clenched with sorrow as a wave of sadness washed over her. Zac, now a haunting echo of the man he once was, lying amid the petals and thorns.

Barkley's plaintive whine pierced through the heavy silence. He nudged her shin with his nose, as if urging her to do something. She offered the dog a reassuring rub of his head.

"Ponsonby!" Mary called out, not realizing her loyal butler was right next to her. Dotty and Margie approached, seemingly from nowhere, and shrieked. Winnie came up last and spied the scene impassively.

"Shh, Barkley," Mary murmured, gently hushing the dog's yipping with a soft pat. She cast a quick glance around, ensuring that their commotion hadn't attracted unwanted attention from the guests. *The last thing I need is to cause a scene amid the festivities.*

"Easy now," Mary instructed the girls, her voice calm. "Let's not disturb the guests with ... our discovery."

Mary pushed aside her apprehensions, focusing instead on maintaining the illusion of tranquility. *After all, the show must go on, even in the face of tragedy.*

"I don't think there's anything we can do to prevent disturbing the party, my lady," Ponsonby said, leaning over the body with an eagle eye on the crime scene.

"We must summon the police," Winnie declared, her chin up and her hands resting on her hips.

"Dotty and I will go entertain the guests and keep them distracted until the authorities arrive," Margie said, and gently pulled on Dotty's arm, urging her from her trance, to follow.

With a shared nod of understanding, the two girls set off toward the terrace.

Mary felt a slight whim of satisfaction as the young ladies took responsibility and Barkley rumbled contentedly.

Ponsonby stooped down to examine the body, while Winnie peered over his shoulder like an astute investigator. "Still warm," he said, turning over the body to study the young gardener's dung-covered face. Ponsonby turned the head and leaned closer to inspect the dirt around Tamberton's mouth and nose. He grimaced, posturing back to a respectable stiffness. "I'm afraid, my lady—"

"Appears he suffocated in the compost," Winnie interrupted.

"Suffocated?" Mary asked with disbelief. "Goodness, how dreadful."

Ponsonby's professional demeanor remained unruffled. "Yes, indeed. Poor Mr. Tamberton has met an unfortunate end."

Mary nodded solemnly, her brow knitted and her mind racing, as she struggled to make sense of the situation. "But perhaps it was simply a matter of natural causes," she suggested tentatively, clinging to the hope that her gardener's death wasn't the result of foul play.

Ponsonby regarded her with an arched eyebrow, his expression betraying his skepticism. "Natural causes, my lady? Amid a busy party. His face forced down into compost? He appears to have inhaled some. It's in his mouth and nose. He wasn't dead before he fell into the compost. Someone held him there."

"It's still possible," Mary insisted, though her voice lacked conviction. "He may have become unconscious and fallen face down, not able to save himself." *This is the third death during our charge over the last year.*

"Well, stranger things *have* happened, Lady Mary," Winnie quipped before leaving them.

"Perhaps he met his demise from an overdose of snuff and

landed here?" Ponsonby's lips twitched in amusement, a subtle glimmer of mirth dancing in his eyes and the hint of a smile tugging at the corners of his mouth. And as quickly as she witnessed it, his countenance turned serious once more. "A creative theory," Ponsonby murmured with a bow. "I'll see that the authorities receive prompt notification."

* * * * * * * * * *

THE PARTY BUZZED in the background, a symphony of laughter and clinking glasses, as Mary hovered like a sentinel over Zac. Ponsonby had excused himself to make the call, leaving her to grapple with the unsettling reality of the situation.

The police arrived too quickly, and Mary's heart sank as Inspector Leonard Fletcher strode toward her, exuding an air of authority that bordered on disdain. His neatly trimmed mustache stressed his stern posture.

I've not heard good things about this inspector. A bead of sweat formed on Mary's brow.

Clad in a crisply pressed suit of deep charcoal gray, he donned a matching fedora, tilted at just the right angle, with a touch of gray peppering his dark hair. His polished leather shoes clicked against the garden path with each purposeful step in her direction. When he approached, his sharp gaze swept over the scene, and his lips pressed into a thin line of disapproval. He hovered over Mary, his broad frame giving him a commanding presence, while uniformed officers fanned out across the lawn and onto the terrace.

"Duchess," Fletcher greeted her, his voice brimming with suspicion. "I trust you can explain this... unfortunate event?"

She squared her shoulders but poised herself gracefully in her floral-patterned dress, perfectly tailored for the summer garden party. With a warm smile and a genteel manner, she greeted him, "Inspector." She met Fletcher's gaze. "I assure you, I can't. I had no hand in this tragedy."

Fletcher's lips curled into a sardonic smile. "Of course," he retorted, his tone dripping with sarcasm. "But forgive me if I find it difficult to believe that such a convenient demise occurred under your watch."

Mary's jaw tightened at the thinly veiled accusation. *Is he seriously accusing me?* "Inspector Fletcher," she countered, her voice firm. "I assure you, Zaclan's death is as much a shock to me as it is to anyone else. There was no foul play on my part, and it's anything but convenient." *I won't allow this inspector to tarnish my name or legacy.*

Before Fletcher responded, the three young sleuths reunited and flitted into the garden, their enthusiasm bursting forth like curious butterflies. Ignoring the gravity of the situation, they peppered the inspector with questions and theories.

"Inspector, do you think the rose bed holds the key to the mystery?" Dotty asked, her eyes sparkling.

"Or perhaps the soil has some hidden clues?" Margie chimed in.

Winnie said, in a measured tone, "Maybe we should interrogate the guests, Inspector. I'm sure one of them must know something!"

Fletcher's glance remained stern, his patience obviously wearing thin. *Are the young ladies' antics aggravating him?* Mary delighted in that his facial attempts to maintain order fell flat.

Mary watched with amusement and exasperation, grateful for the distraction provided by her spirited companions. Yet, as the inspector attempted to shut down the girls' inquisition, his focus quickly shifted back to Mary.

"Enough!" Fletcher boomed. "This is no time for idle speculation and childish games. We're dealing with a serious matter here."

The girls, chastened by Fletcher's stern reprimand, fell silent and then exchanged sheepish glances among themselves. Mary suppressed a smile, knowing full well the irrepressible nature of her young friends. *Nice try Inspector, you're no match for these three ladies.*

His gaze was cold and unyielding. "Well, Duchess," he said, his tone dripping with disdain.

"Inspector Fletcher. I've already assured you of *my* innocence. You haven't been on the scene long enough to have evidence to the contrary. I suggest you focus your efforts on the crime scene." She waved her arm toward the dead body.

With narrowed eyes and a clenched jaw, the inspector barely concealed a spit of anger. "I know your type," he snapped. "Always hiding behind your privilege and influence. But mark my words, I will uncover the truth, no matter how hard you try to conceal it."

Conceal the truth? He can't be far from it himself. I won't let his bias against me cloud his judgment or blind him to the real culprit lurking—at my garden party.

Internally, she seethed with frustration. *I have no faith in this inspector's ability to uncover the truth!*

6

UNEARTHING SECRETS

After corralling her three amateur sleuths, Mary stood to the side with them while Fletcher inspected the crime scene.

With a brisk stride, Fletcher approached Zac's lifeless form lying amid the soil of the flower bed. His keen eyes swept the area, taking in every detail with meticulous scrutiny.

First, he knelt beside the body, his fingers gloved as he carefully examined the soil beneath Zac. With pursed lips, he jotted notes on a small pad. Next, Fletcher leaned in closer, his nostrils flaring as he inhaled deeply. With a precise move he lifted Zac's limp hand, inspecting the underside of his fingernails. Finally, Fletcher rose to his feet and straightened up, his bearing inscrutable as he slipped his notepad back into his breast pocket.

Facing Mary, he started in on her again. "Well, Duchess." He drew out her title with condescension. "I can't help but wonder if this party of yours was merely a smokescreen, a cleverly orchestrated charade to *bring about* . . ." he paused, then threw up his hand, ". . . or even to *cover up* this poor gardener's death."

Mary recoiled at the audacity of the accusation, her eyes

grew round with disbelief. "Inspector, that's preposterous! Zaclan was a friend. I've known him and his family for years. Why would I want to kill him? Besides, I would never stoop to such deceitful measures."

"Forgive me if I find it difficult to take your word at face value, Duchess," he retorted. "Given your track record of deaths popping up around you, I'm inclined to believe that there's more to this than meets the eye."

"Inspector, I assure you—" she began, but Fletcher cut her off with a dismissive wave of his hand.

"Save your protests. I intend to sort this out, with or without your cooperation. And mark my words, Duchess—the truth will come out."

Yes, it certainly will, Inspector Fletcher. *And we'll likely find it before you do.*

Just as Mary felt overwhelmed, Ponsonby materialized by her side. With a grateful sigh, Mary turned her attention away from the inspector.

Behind her, the trio of young sleuths fidgeted, their restless energy almost tangible. Mary sensed their eagerness.

As Inspector Fletcher strode away, leaving the group with his accusations, he paused, casting a last glance over his shoulder. "And one more thing, Duchess, I also knew Zac, the victim, well. We shared a passion for gardening, you see. This investigation is personal for me, and I intend to see justice served for my comrade."

Could it be that Fletcher's connection to Zac will cloud his judgment, drive him to pursue his own agenda at any cost?

Internally, Mary speculated about the inspector's background. *I assume he must come from a humble upbringing, unlike Zac himself. And perhaps, in Fletcher's eyes, Zac's fall from the high station he was born into, to the lowly workmanlike position he was now filling made him a target. But for what?*

Leaving no time for Mary to dwell on her thoughts, Fletcher hailed them all to follow him. The police officers' arrival had punctuated the solemn atmosphere, and they swiftly moved forward to contain the crime scene. Inspector Fletcher wasted no time in directing everyone with authoritative commands.

Fletcher turned to Mary, Ponsonby and the girls. "We need to question your guests, Duchess," he declared, his tone leaving no room for argument. "Especially those who may have had contact with the deceased this afternoon."

Mary nodded, her mind already racing to identify potential witnesses among the partygoers. "Well, Inspector, we had just finished a small tour of the gardens. Perhaps we should start with those guests."

"Very well," Fletcher said. "I want you to be there at the terrace when I speak to them." He pointed toward the terrace where all her guests were at the balustrade watching the police activity.

"Would you like me to explain why you're here, Inspector?" Mary asked, as she set off walking beside Fletcher. Ponsonby fell into step beside Mary. Dressed in his customary attire of a tailored, black suit, with a crisp, white shirt and polished shoes, Ponsonby exuded an air of quiet authority that commanded her respect, and, she hoped, Inspector Fletcher's as well.

"That won't be necessary, Duchess," Fletcher replied, ending any further discussion.

At Mary's side trotted Barkley, his ears perked; he remained vigilant, his nose twitching as he sniffed the air.

Beside Mary, Ponsonby, and Barkley, the trio of young sleuths kept pace, each with their own distinct energy. Winnie, the rational leader of the three, paced ahead with a determined stride. Together, they formed a formidable band of investigators, united in a desire for the truth. *We'll get there before* Inspector Fletcher *with his conventional detection methods!*

This small party with Inspector Fletcher climbed the steps onto the terrace as behind them the police officers searched around the garden. Mary scanned the crowd of guests, until her eyes settled on a cluster of friends she wanted to speak with. *There's no hiding this from the guests now.*

Inspector Fletcher pulled her aside. "Duchess, I can't help but wonder about your butler's involvement in this matter. He seems very protective, too much so. Is it possible he's become jealous of the head gardener's growing influence over you?"

Mary stepped backward in disbelief at yet another of Fletcher's wild accusations. "Inspector! Ponsonby is a loyal servant. He would never harm a fly, let alone Zaclan. You're grasping at straws! If you're seeking a motive, perhaps you should consider the snuff business. Zaclan dabbled in it, and there are plenty of people, even here today, who might stoop so low to gain control of such a lucrative enterprise."

Fletcher's brow furrowed at Mary's suggestion. "A motive," he murmured. "I'll make note."

With a nod, Fletcher focussed back on the investigation. *Though I have a feeling that the truth is lurking just beyond our reach. How will we get around this inspector's accusations?*

Just then, one police officer took Ponsonby by the arm. "Unhand my butler," Mary argued. "He's done nothing to warrant such treatment."

"Step aside Madam," the officer barked. "We're only questioning him in connection with the murder of Zac Tamberton, nothing more—yet."

"Inspector, this is highly irregular. I can't understand your methods," Mary protested, and all attention from the party was now focused on them.

This is disastrous.

"Let us do our jobs," Fletcher responded, signaling the officers to take Ponsonby away. "You'll get him back if he's done nothing wrong. Meanwhile, he knows everything that goes on around here, so at the very least he'll be a key witness."

"But you're treating him like a suspect," Mary cried. "What reason do you have for doing that?"

"By his own admission, he tampered with the body," Fletcher replied. "With your so-called knowledge of these matters, you and he should have known better. I have to assume he might have done that to hide evidence. And that leads me back to him or, with his misplaced feudal loyalty, to you."

"This is ridiculous, Inspector," Mary said. "As I'm sure you know. Frightening us to get a confession won't work here. Neither I nor Ponsonby killed Zaclan."

"Then you and he have nothing to fear. Your butler will return in time to serve you dinner this evening," Fletcher replied, barely concealing his contempt.

"With this attitude," Mary responded, "I doubt we'll ever find the true killer."

"My attitude is based on years of experience in these matters," Fletcher replied, moving away. "I know your man likely felt he was acting in the best interests of you and your family name, but murder is murder. I assure you, we'll have the truth out of him before your party is over."

Mary steadied herself, knowing anger would make things worse. "Inspector, Ponsonby, and I have been mingling with our guests almost every minute this afternoon. He has had no opportunity to kill Zaclan. There are fifty witnesses here to confirm that."

Fletcher's smile in response was positively sinister. "I think you'll find, Duchess, when you do your inevitable snooping, your butler was *not* in view of everyone the whole time. He too assured us he was, but we have witnesses who saw him leave and return only after they heard you calling for him."

"He was in the kitchen ensuring refreshments were on their

way," Mary cried. "Or in the wine cellar, ensuring the staff there were using the right wines. He has an important job and can't always be on the terrace."

Grinning, Fletcher continued, "You and he need to manage your stories better. First you say he was in full view of everyone all the time, and now you say he was away sometimes. Which is it?"

Mary didn't want to get into an argument and asked, "Have you questioned the kitchen or wine cellar staff? They will confirm where he was."

"If he was as innocent as you say," Fletcher replied, "I'm sure they would, but they were busy people and couldn't be sure. How is it you are so sure, Duchess?"

"Because I know him! I will do everything I can to prove his innocence!" Mary shouted at the retreating inspector's back.

The inspector stopped, turned, and asked, "And where were you, Duchess? Perhaps, you can think about that before I return to continue the interviews."

7

TEA, TIDBITS, AND TALES

Mary, the three girls, and Barkley, watched in stunned disbelief as officers marched Ponsonby away in handcuffs to a police car. Mary's heart pounded in her chest, her hands trembling.

"Is this really necessary, Inspector?" But her argument received a cold shoulder; the only response was the hollow thud of the door slamming shut. Her steadfast right-hand man, now sat locked away, cut off from her in the blink of an eye. She watched as Fletcher, without even replying, strode off into the house to continue interviewing her guests.

Mary stood there, frozen, her eyes returning to the police car as it pulled out of the entrance gates and turned onto the road and out of sight. Helplessness surged within her. *How did it come to this? How could someone as devoted as Ponsonby—whose entire life revolves around order and dignity—possibly be implicated in something so dark?*

"Why do they think Ponsonby had something to do with it?" Dotty asked, bewildered.

Winnie scowled. "They've only just arrived and they haven't

had time to gather *any* evidence against *anyone*, let alone poor Ponsonby."

"The inspector said he thought Ponsonby may have grown jealous regarding Zaclan's influence over me," Mary replied bitterly. "And when we found the body, Ponsonby turned Zaclan over and examined his nose and mouth. The inspector thinks Ponsonby was destroying evidence."

"But that's nonsense," Margie said. "Zac is only a gardener, and only for the laying out of the new gardens. How could his influence have pushed Ponsonby aside? And as for touching the body, well, words fail me."

"That man has a bee in his bonnet about the aristocracy and their servants, I fear," Mary answered. "He's not even met any of us prior."

"Certainly not you, at least," Dotty agreed. "Not all the aristocracy is as kind and welcoming as you, Lady Mary."

"The inspector will have to release Ponsonby because there's no evidence," Margie declared. "In case he doesn't, we should gather evidence to get Ponsonby released sooner rather than later."

Throwing her hands on her hips, Winnie argued, "The police are preventing us from getting anywhere near the crime scene, so collecting physical evidence is out of the question, and we can't interview the guests because the officers won't allow that either."

Dotty shook her head. "But we know something they don't." She waited, watching as the others leaned in with curiosity. "There was your nosey neighbor, Quiggly Smythe, wandering the grounds before and during the event. He isn't here now, so where did he go?"

Mary leaned forward, her eyes lit up with sudden insight. "You saw him too?" she asked, watching Dotty closely as she nodded, though her expression remained puzzled.

"What is it, dear?" Mary pressed.

Dotty hesitated, glancing down as if piecing things together. "I've just realized I assumed it was him," she admitted, a faint wrinkle forming between her brows. "I didn't see his face or anything. But who else could it be?"

"Nobody else," Mary said with certainty, straightening her posture. "He's always sneaking around my property. Yet, with all that's happened, I'd quite forgotten about him. Well done, Dotty. You're far more astute than anyone gives you credit for."

Margie, already shifting her weight from foot to foot, sighed impatiently. Her foot now tapped anxiously on the driveway. "We should spread out and search."

Mary nodded. "You three do that," she agreed, already turning to go back into the house. "But I'll need to settle the guests' nerves after all this excitement. They won't be pleased at being caught up in a murder investigation."

Her three assistants spun to leave too, but she stopped them. "Ladies, please be sensible. If you see Mr. Smythe, do not approach him or try to question him. Follow him if you can without being seen. If he truly is involved in Zaclan's death, he may kill again to escape capture."

Winnie cocked her head, her curtain of sleek hair moving with the action. "I don't think he could've killed Zaclan on his own. He's a weedy middle-aged man, and the gardener was strong. He could've easily just thrown your neighbor off if the weasel tried to hold Zaclan's face in the manure."

"And?" Margie questioned. "Why was Zac at the rose bed, anyway? We all went to change, and wasn't he supposed to take care of something quickly and rejoin us all on the terrace when he'd done the same?"

"Then you've plenty of questions that need answers and clues to keep an eye out for," Mary said, waving them away. She finished with, "And not just nosey neighbors."

The three hurried off, and Mary made her way through the house and returned to the terrace where her guests were complaining bitterly, as she'd suspected they would.

"Jolyon's been taken to the library for questioning," Lord Abernoothy said, an angry scowl on his face. "He'll be terrified. You know how the police are with people like Jolyon."

Mary responded, speaking to the entire group. "They won't leave until we are all questioned. They need to note our testimonies now, lest we forget pertinent details. Keep calm, and tell them exactly what you know. The ordeal will pass quicker that way, I promise."

"But we know nothing," the Duchess of Mothford cried, wiping perspiration from her brow with a delicate handkerchief. "I didn't even go on the garden tour. I can't tell them anything of importance."

"Your questioning should be very brief, and you'll soon be back here sipping champagne before you know it," Mary replied, with what she hoped was a reassuring smile.

I wish I could be this reassured about Ponsonby. What did the inspector mean when he said no one can vouch for his time. Or my time? Where was I?

"I'm not drinking another drop of alcohol until they've gone," Abernoothy said, digging his heels in and crossing his arms. "I don't want them twisting my words and trying to pin this death on me, or one of us, you'll see. We must keep our heads clear."

She wasn't entirely sure why he thought his account would get twisted, but he continued interrupting her thoughts. "The SNUF Society. We're all in it, and so was Zac." He threw his hand out as if vindicating his own statements.

Mary stopped herself from rolling her eyes. "But snuff isn't a banned substance, and the Society isn't an illegal organization. You're making something out of nothing, Abernoothy."

"You mark my words," he huffed, then turned his back on them, saying over his shoulder, "they'll link his death to us." Then he walked away.

What does he know that makes him so sure of that? Might he have more to do with the case than we know?

The group broke into fractious low whispering that Mary could see was mainly to support this preposterous idea. "I'm sure Lord Abernoothy is mistaken about what might happen, but I agree that, until you've told them what you know, not drinking is a sensible idea. I'll have coffee, tea, and additional foods brought out while we wait."

She left the group and went in search of Cook, having spied her out of the corner of her eye, at the far end of the terrace with the three girls.

Mary almost reached them when the corgi raced past Mary and joined the young sleuths. Mary continued walking until she reached Cook, who was with the group discussing who would go where. Cook was dithering about whom to follow when she declared, "I must keep those three in line."

Barkley puttered around Dotty's heels and gripped her pant leg.

"Barkley," Dotty yelled, bending to stroke him. "Where've you been?"

The plump corgi gently bit the cuff of her boy-jeans, tugged at them, and let out a low growl. When he let go, Dotty dutifully followed, calling out to the others, "Barkley and I will head toward the shrubbery. You all choose your own ways."

"Dotty's right. We need to cover as much ground as we can and not all go one way. I'll take the property boundary where the neighbor might have entered and left from," Winnie instructed.

"Then Cook and I will go back to the terrace and search there around to the front of the house and drive," Margie replied. "We know Smythe was there this morning when he spoke to Lady Mary. Maybe he came and went that way this afternoon too."

Cook paused as if to take direction from Mary instead.

"Wonderful plan, but I'll go with you, Margie. Cook you're needed in the kitchen, if you would please. Post haste." She relayed the requirement for non-alcoholic refreshments to Cook, who nodded and took her leave without question.

Mary hurried back to the terrace where she was pleased to see a relieved Sir Jolyon had returned. Winnie's father was missing, presumably in the library being interviewed by Inspector Fletcher.

"Refreshments are on their way." Mary passed the word to be spread among guests. "Now, everyone, let's make the best of what's left of this awful afternoon."

It took some time before she could leave the terrace. Everyone wanted to have Mary understand their feelings about the awful event. Mary felt she would scream if she couldn't soon disentangle herself from the crowd but, just as she was losing all hope, a police constable came from the house with Winnie's father. The two men joined Winnie's mother who was then escorted by the officer into the house.

Winnie's father was now the center of everyone's attention, and Mary made her escape, only to find Margie had left without her. Mary peered about, hoping to see Margie but saw instead, Barkley at the edge of the line of bushes that Zac had recently planted. She set off in pursuit of Barkley, hurrying to catch up, and soon saw him with Dotty.

Trailing behind Dotty and Barkley, Mary entered a grove of young trees.

"What is it, Barkley?" Mary heard Dotty gasp.

The dog snuffled at something among the undergrowth, then gave Dotty one of his penetrating 'don't you know' stares.

As Mary arrived at her side, Dotty grabbed a stick and picked up the object Barkley had found. To Mary, it appeared to be a glove. *It is like any other glove, and certainly not something to get too excited about.* Barkley wagged his rump.

"Do you think it's important?" Dotty asked the dog.

Barkley yipped repeatedly, in what they could only assume was confirmation.

Mary pushed up on her tiptoes to get a better look over the slender girl's shoulder.

Dotty shrugged, holding it out like something rotten, clearly not sure of the glove's worth as evidence.

"It might be evidence," Mary said. "You'll have to take that to the police."

Dotty nodded, and they set off with Barkley proudly leading the way. Dotty, however, just looked embarrassed.

Smiling, Mary tried not to laugh at the comical figure Dotty presented while carrying the discarded glove at the end of a stick all the way back to the terrace.

The young lady's ambivalence to the glove turned out to be half-right. While Mary had been mildly interested, Inspector Fletcher gave the glove only a passing glance.

"Give that to one of my constables, and have him add it into the evidence log," he said, then hurried off to his next interview.

The corgi quirked his nose as if in approval of the instructions.

"Must be the scent on the glove," Mary replied. "Maybe, if we let Barkley sniff it again, he can lead us to the owner."

Dotty cast Mary a thoughtful glance and asked, "What about the police?"

"We'll hand it over when we have finished our hunt," Mary replied, and took the stick from Dotty, who breathed a deep sigh of relief. Mary held the glove to the dog's nose. *I hope this works.*

"Seek, Barkley," Mary commanded, straightening up.

His attention caught by a police dog in the distance, Barkley stopped, huffed, then set off. The dog scampered in the direction where the glove had been lying around the shrubs and then barked aggressively before dropping his nose to the ground and sniffing around. They followed the barking Barkley beyond the row of shrubs, across the lawn, and past the crime scene. There, he continued to sniff around for a length of time, and Mary worried that he'd lost the scent until, with a yip of triumph, he set off racing toward the estate boundary to the north, where Winnie had gone.

"It *must be* your nosey neighbor's glove," Dotty exclaimed.

"Well, its owner certainly came from there," Mary agreed, puffing a little at the pace the stout little dog forced upon them. "However, anyone could've climbed over the fence from his property. Not a definitive clue to his guilt."

Arriving at the fence that separated the Snodsbury estate from its neighbor, Barkley turned and plopped his rump down, sitting triumphantly as Dotty and the duchess arrived.

Mary smiled. "Somebody came this way and hid in the shrubbery today. You can tell by the bent and broken branches." She patted the dog on the head. "Well done." She examined a scraped fence post and trodden down wire. "It appears they were in a hurry at this point."

"If the culprit had just killed Zac, they'd definitely be in a rush to get away," Dotty said grimly. "I hope he hangs when they catch him."

Mary looked along the fence, thinking she might see Winnie who had set out to examine this area of the garden, but there was no one in sight.

Correctly divining what Mary was doing, Dotty said, "Winnie will have passed here ages ago."

"It seems so," Mary agreed. "Without Barkley's clever nose to point at the disturbance, she probably thought it was how the place normally looks."

Dotty laughed. "It *is* hard to tell weeds brushed aside by the wind or by animals, from weeds pushed aside by a fleeing human."

"You need a Barkley nose, it's true."

Led by the corgi, the two walked back to the house, where they handed over the glove, as requested, and told the police constable what they had discovered. He quickly found a sergeant, and a police dog with a handler, to retrace the route Mary described to him.

Howling, Barkley obviously took exception. When he began growling at the German Shepherd, the tracking dog peered down its long nose at the corgi.

Let's see how good this *dog is. I'm sure he'll find nothing more than Barkley did.*

8

BONES OF CONTENTION

Next on the scene, a senior police officer arrived with an elderly man in a wrinkled overcoat. *Is this a doctor who has been down on his luck, maybe?*

His coat flapped around him as he bustled about. "Dr. Carmichael." He muttered the announcement to no one in particular. "Police pathologist." He carried a heavy leather case, and his eyebrows furrowed in irritation. "Honestly," he said to himself, his voice rising, "rushing all the way out to Snodsbury for this nonsense. Delivering autopsy reports in person—what a waste of my time."

Mary caught his eye, and offered a polite smile. "Dr. Carmichael, is it? Welcome to Snodsbury. I assume you're here for Inspector Fletcher?"

"Yes, yes," he replied, waving a hand dismissively. "Where is he? I haven't got all day. Had to drop everything to get here, you know. Autopsies don't complete themselves."

Mary raised an eyebrow but kept her composure. As they walked, Dr. Carmichael continued to grumble. "Should've been done by phone. What do they think we are? Delivery boys?"

Mary bit back a retort. "I'm sure Inspector Fletcher will appreciate your efforts, Doctor."

"Yes, well," he said, adjusting his glasses, "he'd better."

"Here we are," Mary said, delivering the man to the inspector.

"Surely you'll share the details with me once you've reviewed the findings of the good doctor here?"

Fletcher hesitated, his lips pressing into a tight line. "This is official police business, Lady Mary. I'm not at liberty to—"

Mary's eyes narrowed slightly as she cut him off. "I understand such, Inspector, but you might recall that the Chief Constable himself was among my guests. I doubt he'd appreciate learning that I've been kept in the dark about a murder investigation occurring right here on my own grounds."

Fletcher's expression shifted, a hint of discomfort flashing across his face. With a nod, he reached for the report. "Fine," he conceded. "But this information stays between us."

Fletcher read the report, his eyes darting down the page. He then handed it to Mary.

"I'd assumed Mr. Tamberton had to be drugged," Mary said as she finished reading. "Everyone at the party was too old to have held him down."

Shifting uncomfortably, Fletcher said, "Your dog's discovery earlier, a clever little fellow I have to say, leads me to think the murderer wasn't at the party." He cleared his throat. "It was someone who came onto the property to meet the victim or maybe just to *murder* the victim, though how he could have known the victim would go out into the grounds alone, I can't yet see. Or why the victim was out there at all. He was to rejoin you all on the terrace after he changed into dry clothes."

"Not quite, Inspector," Mary replied. "Zac told the girls he had something he wanted to do before rejoining everyone on the terrace. They thought he was going to discover who had soaked them all."

Fletcher nodded. "I remember. Maybe the girls can remember more if I speak to them again. Likely, they know or saw something that would explain his presence among the roses."

"Does that mean the remaining guests can leave, Inspector?" Mary asked. "They all have long journeys, and none of them are young people."

"Not yet, please. Our questioning yesterday was all about the garden party and the other guests," Fletcher replied. "I'd like to ask those who remain if they saw someone they didn't know at the party. We might get a surprising answer. Sometimes people don't realize what they know until asked directly."

"After that, can they go? Many are eager to leave, and I want to give them some hope."

Fletcher nodded. "Yes, tell them that. The update may make them readier to answer my questions."

"Inspector, this drug the report mentions: Chloral Hydrate. Is it quick-acting?" Mary said, puzzled.

"Under the manure, the pathologist found traces of it on the victim's lips," Fletcher replied. "He has yet to determine if that caused the victim the inability to fight back. As to the speed of its action, that depends on the dose and how it's taken. Fifteen minutes is possible, in some circumstances, I believe."

Mary shook her head frowning. "There was barely time from Zaclan being seen leaving the terrace and his body being found for a normal sedative to act. Maybe it was longer than fifteen minutes, but not a lot more."

"I believe it more incapacitates, than sedates," Fletcher replied. "Possibly Mr. Tamberton was simply drowsy and unable to defend himself, rather than unconscious."

Her eyes widened in horror. "You mean he was still conscious when he was being smothered?"

Fletcher nodded, his lips pressed into a straight line, his eyes downcast. "I'm afraid so. A nasty way to go." He shook his head.

"How awful. From the description of particles in his lungs I understood him to be alive and breathing but assumed he was at least unconscious."

"There's no need to tell anyone else that detail," Fletcher replied, holding out his hand for the report. "Particularly your young friends. You'll give them nightmares."

Mary silently agreed with Fletcher. She shifted to go, saying, "I'll call everyone together and explain what you need from them, Inspector. When you're ready to start, we'll all be in the drawing room."

Only some of her guests had stayed the night because of their long journey home, and they were already in the breakfast room. Gathering them for a meeting was easy. She only had to tell those who were still eating breakfast to meet in the drawing room at ten and bring anyone who hadn't yet made it down to breakfast with them.

It was a subdued group that Mary surveyed when the appointed time arrived. They sat around her as she hovered, by the eighteenth century Adam fireplace, waiting to hear their fate for the day.

Putting on a brave smile, Mary said, "I have some good news."

The group's reaction was slight, barely acknowledging her positivity—remaining sullen instead.

"Inspector Fletcher says he has only a few more questions for each of you, then you can return to your homes." Had she expected rapturous joy upon hearing this, she would've felt disappointed. As it was, she was not.

"We spent all yesterday with the inspector and his questions," Lord Abernoothy said, a pipe dangling from his pouting lips. "What more can he want to know?"

"He has additional evidence that suggests a different possibility, and he needs to know what you may have seen that would confirm such." Mary smiled. "It should only take a short time and then you can go."

The group returned once again to silently staring at her as though they blamed her for the unpleasantness. Fortunately, before it became too oppressive, a police constable entered the room and called for Lady Mothford to accompany him to the interview room. This broke the ice, and slowly, stilted conversations began, and grew, until everything was normal again.

True to his word, Inspector Fletcher didn't keep any of them long, and by half-past noon, the last of her guests were ready to leave. The SNUF Society men were in such good humor that they stayed for a long, hearty lunch. Which worked in Mary's favor.

As they dawdled over their port, Mary asked, "Would the SNUF Society welcome a visit from me? Do you let outsiders into your hallowed halls?"

"Of course we do," Abernoothy said. "We welcome anyone with an interest in snuff. Has this weekend made you curious?"

"Not exactly," Mary admitted. "Still, I can't shake the feeling that Zaclan's death might be in connection with his dabbling in snuff and the new recipes he created."

Steele laughed. "Be sensible, Mary. It's snuff, powdered tobacco, and our club isn't a drug cartel headquarters, or whatever else you might think it is."

Mary flushed. "I don't mean that. Only there aren't many motives that I can see for his death. My landscaping project, while beautiful, isn't the stuff of murderous intent either. His many relationships may hold a clue or two, but none of his girlfriends were here."

"I'd leave that to the police, Mary." Abernoothy waved dismissively. "Not your concern, old girl."

"He was *my* gardener, killed on *my* estate, at *my* garden party," Mary hissed out, a little sharper than she had intended. "That makes it *my* concern. And I know his family. I can't just let the police bungle it. If another murder occurs, they'll lose focus and shift their attention, and before long, everyone will forget about Zaclan."

"Another murder," Steele scoffed. "This is Norfolk, Mary. That would be in the next decade, not a month."

"Will one of you invite and escort me to the next meeting?" Mary demanded, determined not to be brushed aside.

"Of course, we will," Abernoothy said, puffing on his pipe. "Just don't imagine you're going to find clues there. We're the quietest bunch of people you'll ever meet."

"Duchess," the inspector called, and she turned to face the sound of his voice. He was outside the room she'd made available to the police for additional interviews and calling the full length of the hall. "Do you have a minute?"

Mary would have liked to snub him or demand he request an interview with one of her staff, but she knew either course of action would only confirm his prejudice against her and her class.

"Certainly, Inspector," she replied, with an icy smile, and went to join him.

"The Chief Constable says I'm to treat you with respect," Fletcher told her, as she took a seat opposite him. "I assured him I treat everyone with the same degree of respect. I don't play favorites." He grinned, his smile as icy as Mary's had been.

She mirrored the expression. "I'm sure you do your best, Inspector."

"I try to. Now, in the matter I alluded to earlier. Where were you when your gardener was being killed?"

"I don't know when Zaclan's death took place exactly, Inspector," Mary replied.

"Nor does anyone except the murderer, Duchess. You and your dog found the body, and yet, no one remembers seeing you leave the party."

Mary bit her lip as she gathered her thoughts. "I'd stepped aside from the terrace for a moment..."

"Why?"

Mary shook her head in exasperation. "I felt like it, Inspector. Don't you ever just want a moment's respite from the noise? Even a cheerful noise like a party?"

Fletcher shrugged. "I don't go to parties."

No one would be mad enough to invite you to their party. "Well, if you did, Inspector, you might take a moment to quiet your mind," Mary said, irritably. "I'd only been on the steps beside the terrace a few minutes when Barkley rushed up and demanded I go with him."

"A talking dog, that'll go down well in the witness box," Fletcher remarked.

"You don't have a dog, either, I take it, Inspector."

"I don't. Dirty, noisy creatures," he replied.

Mary calmed herself, before saying, "If you had, you'd know what they're trying to tell you, particularly when they're as agitated as Barkley was."

"So, you followed him."

"I did, and found Zaclan as you saw." Mary replied.

"Not quite as I saw, though, was he Duchess," Fletcher said. "You and, or, your butler interfered with the corpse before I arrived."

"Ponsonby checked to see if he was alive, that's all."

"He didn't perhaps check the deceased's pockets?" Fletcher asked.

"Certainly not."

"Anything else I should know about?"

"Nothing. The girls had already gone back to the terrace, and I waited with Zac while Ponsonby went to call the police. That's all."

"Was your gardener much of a drinker?" Fletcher asked, surprising Mary with this change of subject.

"You knew him too, Inspector," Mary replied. "Did you think he was one?"

Fletcher looked puzzled. "I didn't, but seeing someone for an hour a month at the local gardening club hardly equals knowing someone that well."

Mary nodded. "I think he hardly drank at all, Inspector, but like you, I had a limited relationship with him to certain subjects. Young men often drink more than they should, I believe. Was he intoxicated?"

Fletcher shook his head. "We have a witness who saw him," he read from his notes, "'toss off a mixed drink like it was a habit with him.'"

"I didn't see him with a glass in his hand at all," Mary replied, as puzzled as Fletcher. "When was this?"

"The witness wasn't sure, unfortunately."

"Well, I can't help you with that. Were the girls able to add more to what they'd told you before?"

"I'm afraid not," Fletcher replied. "Even the bit about him going to discover who had operated the sprinkler was their idea, not something he said."

"I can't think of anything that I haven't already told you, Inspector, but I assure you, if I do, you will be the first to know."

"Very well," Fletcher said. "That will be all—for now." He closed his notebook with an aggressive snap and gestured Mary to leave.

Mary left, her mind boiling with rage. *What a self-important, arrogant little man. How dare he? If this is the 'respect' he shows everyone, I can't imagine how an ordinary man or woman might feel after such an interview.* It was the middle of the night before she was calm enough for sleep.

LORD ABERNOOTHY HAD BEEN RIGHT. The SNUF Society emergency meeting two days later, called to commemorate Zac's death and discuss his new recipes, was as somber and slow as an actual funeral.

"Gentlemen," Mary said, in a quiet moment, calling on their attention. "I have a question. Do you think Zaclan's new recipes would be worth anything? Like killing him over?" She peered around the room, scanning facial reactions. "I'd like to be sure they bring his killer to justice, you see. He was a family friend and a wonderful young man. What happened to him is a tragedy."

Members exchanged glances, and one man said, "We all agree with that, Your Grace, but you must understand, we here are the only people for whom those recipes were valuable. However much we may wish it otherwise, in today's world, no one cares about snuff."

She nodded, but couldn't see this old-fashioned practice being the stuff of murder motives either. *But there has to be some motive that made Zac a murder victim. If it wasn't snuff, what was it?*

9

UNEARTHING THE TRUTH

Mary stood on the terrace, a new day in front of her. She had dressed in her favorite peacock-blue brocade dress cinched at the waist with a delicate satin ribbon. The soft breeze carried the sweet scent of roses. Overlooking the expansive gardens of her Snodsbury estate, she watched with a serene smile as the three girls chased Barkley, who was energetically darting after squirrels. The girls' laughter rang out, a cheerful melody that brought a touch of lightness to the otherwise heavy thoughts occupying Mary's mind.

Beside her with one arm folded in front of him, was her trusted butler, his posture impeccable as always.

"There has to be some motive that made our dear gardener a murder victim. If it wasn't for the snuff, though I'm not ruling that out just yet, what was it?"

Ponsonby, who had served the Culpeper family for decades and was privy to many of the estate's secrets, nodded gravely. "Indeed, my lady. Attractive young men have their fair share of admirers, and perhaps even enemies. I feel his charm was undeniable, and charm can often lead to unforeseen complications."

Mary sighed, keeping a sharp eye on things. "If poison

rendered him unconscious, it could be in the snuff. Was his snuffbox on his body when they investigated the scene?"

He paused for a moment. "As I recall, it was not. The constable mentioned the snuffbox was missing, which could show a deliberate theft because that's where the sedative had been placed. And if a sedative was indeed used to incapacitate him, that would suggest someone had intimate knowledge of his habits and would have to be near enough to strike when they saw him take the snuff laced with sedative."

"They had to know his snuff habits at least," Mary mused. "And they had to have access to his snuffbox to adulterate his snuff."

Ponsonby pulled a long face, contemplating the possibilities. "There was a rumor, Your Grace, that Zac was involved with someone of significant standing. Discretion would've been paramount."

"We can't go chasing after gossip. I think we must get this one right the first time." Her thoughts drifted to the last two cases they had investigated, which had led them on several wrong turns. "Zac Tamberton was not only a talented gardener but also an exceptionally attractive young man," she muttered. *His interactions with the various guests were always respectful. Was there ever an undercurrent of something more—any glances or hushed conversations, maybe?*

The scene below shifted as Barkley, in a sudden burst of energy, chased an audacious squirrel who scurried up a tree. The girls, breathless and flushed with excitement, called out to him, their laughter infectious. Mary allowed herself a small smile at their antics before her manner turned serious once more.

"What about his personal relationships?" Mary asked. "Did he confide in anyone here at the estate? Friends? Lovers?"

Ponsonby hesitated. "There were whispers, Your Grace, that

Zac had a fondness for kitchen maids. It might be worth speaking with Cook."

"Yes, we must tread carefully. The last thing we need is to stir up gossip. If Zaclan's death was indeed a result of passion, can we assume it was a woman?"

His lips turned down, Ponsonby shook his head. "While it may likely be a female, we can't assume that any more than the idle gossipers do, my lady."

Mary's mind raced through the possibilities. The missing snuffbox, the potential for a jealous lover, and the intimate nature of the murder all pointed to a carefully orchestrated plan. Someone had wanted Zac dead, and they went to great lengths to ensure this happened discreetly.

"For Zaclan's sake, and for the safety of everyone at Snodsbury, we must uncover the truth. We owe it to him to find out who did this and why."

The butler bowed his head slightly. "As always, my lady, I'm at your service. We shall leave no stone unturned. However, I should mention one uncomfortable thought."

"You mean one of our honored guests?"

Ponsonby ever-so-slightly inclined his head in agreement. "Lord Abernoothy was to go to the victim's room for a half ounce of snuff, if you recall."

Mary nodded "He could've taken some opportunity to place adulterated snuff into Zaclan's snuffbox."

"I fear so, my lady," Ponsonby replied, his face registering as much concern as he could under the circumstances. Lord Abernoothy was a long-standing friend of the family, and it grieved Ponsonby to cast aspersions on the man.

"Did anyone go with them?" Mary asked.

"I didn't see them leave," Ponsonby replied. "Perhaps others did."

"Ask the staff," Mary said. "I'll contact the guests, starting with Abernoothy himself."

With a last glance, Mary sighed. She turned and walked back into the house, her mind already strategizing the next steps.

AN HOUR LATER, her phone calls still not completed, Mary corralled her youthful cohorts on the lawn where they were still enjoying the sunshine. "Dotty, Winnie, and Margie, let's do as Ponsonby has suggested, ladies. Now that the police have gone, we can search and 'leave no stone unturned.'"

The girls nodded eagerly, their previous merriment replaced by a serious determination.

"Come on, girls!" Winnie clapped her hands. "We need to search every inch of this garden. Margie, keep your eyes sharp for anything that seems out of place."

Margie nodded.

"You stay close. No getting distracted, Dotty."

Dotty laughed good-naturedly. "Don't worry, I'll keep up."

They formed a line, with Mary on one end and Winnie on the other. Barkley trotted alongside her eagerly. Margie and Dotty were an arm's length apart in the middle.

They moved methodically through the garden. Mary's heart was heavy with the thought of what they might find. *Could secrets lie buried beneath my garden? Is that the reason behind Zac's death? To stop further digging?*

Barkley darted back and forth, between Winnie and Mary, sniffing at the grasses and bushes.

"Over here!" Winnie called out, crouching near a cluster of rose bushes. She held up a small, shiny object.

The others hurried over, their curiosity piqued. Mary leaned in, peering at the item in Winnie's hand. "What is it?"

"A button," Winnie said, turning it over. "Could be from someone's overcoat."

Dotty frowned. "But is that really a clue? Or just something randomly lost."

Margie took the button and inspected it. "Just a standard black button, nothing particularly special. Let's keep it for now, but I don't think it's the smoking gun we need." She shoved the curio into a pocket of her snug, denim pants.

They continued their search, finding various objects that seemed promising at first but ultimately didn't seem likely to be clues: a torn piece of fabric, an old coin, a child's toy, a ribbon, an old handkerchief, another stray glove, and even a silver pen. Each discovery added to their growing collection, but none provided the breakthrough they'd hoped for.

As they neared the fountain, Mary felt a pang of frustration but maintained positivity for the sake of the team. "We mustn't lose hope. The answer is here somewhere, I can feel it."

Margie raised a reassuring hand, but Mary shot her a pointed glare. She peered down at her dirt-covered fingers and nails and then lowered her hand. "We'll find it, Lady Mary. We just need to keep searching."

Barkley growled suddenly, drawing their attention to a thick shrub near the fountain. He sniffed intently at the base of the shrub, then pawed at the ground.

We're all going to need a proper bath after this adventure.

"What is it, boy?" Dotty asked, hurrying over, her frizzy, ginger curls bouncing. She knelt down and parted the branches where Barkley was pawing the ground, revealing a small leather-bound book. She brushed the soil off the top of it.

Mary's breath caught in her throat. "Could it be . . .?"

Winnie reached in and carefully pulled out the book. "It's a journal," she said, opening the cover. Neat handwriting filled the pages.

Leaning in, Margie appeared to read to herself over Winnie's shoulder. "If that's Zac's penmanship, this could be important."

"Let's take it inside and scrutinize it. This might be his recipe book." Winnie snapped the book shut.

Frowning, Dotty's lazy eye dipped. "Recipes for what? He was a cook also?"

Margie stifled a grimace, and Winnie replied in a flat tone, "Recipes for his snuff, I mean."

Dotty giggled. "Oh, right!"

Once inside, they gathered around a table in the sitting room. Ponsonby entered quietly, his gaze sharpened as it landed on the journal.

"What have you found, my lady?"

Mary sat beside a mid-century floor lamp. "We found a journal hidden near the fountain. We think it's Zaclan's recipes for snuff mixtures."

Ponsonby asked, "How could the police search have missed this? They were all over the garden."

"We don't know," Mary replied. "It was Barkley who found it. I knew he was a better tracker than that police dog they had."

Barkley beamed on hearing his name. His stump of a tail wagged excitedly.

Gathered around her, the girls' flushed faces radiated the thrill of the hunt.

"We found a bunch of other stuff besides, but nothing that screams *motive*," Winnie said, her tone carrying her disappointment. "I imagine that's why the police just left them."

Ponsonby stepped closer. "I thought we'd ruled out his snuff recipes as a motive?"

"Hmm," Mary murmured as she read what was indeed

Zaclan's recipe book—page after page of densely hand-written lines of ingredients. "Maybe."

"Do you think he would've had the time to toss it before being attacked?" Margie asked, bouncing in her seat.

Winnie glared and replied, "Not likely."

"Then he hid it in advance of the garden party," Ponsonby added, "which doesn't seem to make sense."

"Or," Dotty said, her expression thoughtful, "it was the murderer who took it from Zac's pocket and hid it, meaning to come back for it later."

"That makes even less sense, Dotty," Winnie told her. "The murderer would have known the police would search the grounds and find it."

Dotty wasn't in the least taken aback by this. She said, "Or, Zac thought someone attending the garden party might search his room and workplace for the book and hid it himself—somewhere he thought only he could find."

There was a moment's silence as the group considered this.

"You may have something there Dotty, and that takes us back to the SNUF Society," Mary said, handing the book to Winnie who was sitting beside her, waiting.

"It doesn't mean he was killed for it, of course, but it also doesn't rule out snuff or the snuff recipes," Ponsonby whispered. "Perhaps the missing snuffbox is the key. If we can find the box, that might reveal a piece of the puzzle."

Nodding, Mary replied, "We must continue our search, both inside and out. If our dear departed gardener left us breadcrumbs, we just need to follow them to the truth."

10

A ROSE BY ANOTHER NAME

As the afternoon sun began its descent, casting a golden hue over the estate, Mary gathered her resolve. The discovery of the snuff recipe book had ignited a fresh determination within her. She looked to Ponsonby and her trio of eager young sleuths, Dotty, Margie, and Winnie. "We need to search Zaclan's room."

Barkley, sat up in attention.

Mary smiled. "There might be more clues there, perhaps even his snuffbox. Let's not waste any more time."

Ponsonby nodded, his silvery hair slick and his stoic demeanor unwavering. "Very well, my lady. Follow me. However, I fear the police will have taken anything pertinent to the case."

Trotting alongside them, Barkley's nose twitched as if he already sensed the importance of their mission. The group made their way to the servants' quarters.

As they approached Zac's room on the upper floor, they found it blocked by police tape and the door slightly ajar, a sign of the police's recent intrusion. The space in disarray, just as the investigators had left it, drawers were pulled open, and personal items had been strewn about haphazardly. *At least they were thorough in here, even if they weren't while outside in the gardens.*

"Let's be methodical," Mary instructed, her keen eyes scanning the space. "Ponsonby, check the drawers. Dotty, Margie, and Winnie, search for anything unusual. Barkley, please stay close."

With everyone assigned their tasks, the search began in earnest. Ponsonby meticulously went through the drawers, his practiced hands moving with precision. Dotty, Margie, and Winnie examined the scattered papers and belongings, their youthful enthusiasm driving them to diligence.

Mary approached a small writing desk, her fingers brushing over the worn wood. Among the clutter, she noticed a delicate, hand-carved box. *Ah, I found it.* She picked it up, turning the wooden container over in her hands. Intricate decorations, featuring a rose motif that struck her as particularly significant, adorned the top and sides.

"Look at this," Mary said, holding the box up for the others to see, then tried to pry it open with her fingernail. "It's beautiful, and the craftsmanship is exquisite. Why would the police leave this behind?"

The group gathered around, and Mary handed the discovery to the girls to inspect while she looked for Barkley.

Suddenly, the dog whined a low whine, pawing at a pile of discarded bed linens in the corner.

"What is it, Barkley?" Mary asked, hastening to see what had caught the dog's attention. *That's untidy. Which maid left such a mess?*

As she pulled back the sheet, Mary gasped. There, nestled among the fabric, was a pot containing a small plant with fledgling roses unlike any she had ever seen. The uncrushed petals glowed with a deep, velvety red, streaked with gold, creating an otherworldly beauty. The rose's scent intoxicated Mary, blending sweetness and mystery, leaving her momentarily breathless.

"This . . . this is incredible," Mary murmured, gently cupping the pot with one hand. "I've never seen a rose like this. Zaclan must have cultivated it himself. What a masterpiece!"

Ponsonby leaned in, carefully taking the box from her as she picked up the pot. He tilted his head slightly, inspecting the unique flower. "Indeed, my lady. If he did, his gardening prowess is beyond extraordinary."

Dotty, Margie, and Winnie crowded around.

"Do you think someone could've killed him for this rose?" Dotty asked.

"It's possible," Mary replied. "If this rose is as rare and valuable as it appears, it could be worth a fortune. Zaclan's knowledge and skill in cultivating such a plant would make him a target."

The group fell silent.

Winnie scoffed, "Why did the police leave behind the snuffbox?" She pointed to the box Ponsonby held. "And the plant. Don't they know its significance?" She held out her hand, silently seeking the box from the butler. He handed it to her without speaking.

"Maybe because this box has nothing to do with Zaclan or the case," Winnie continued, studying it carefully. "This is empty and looks as if it always has been."

Mary pondered. *The unique rose, the empty snuffbox, the recipe book, and Zac's untimely death. Are they all connected? But how?*

"Let's take this rose to my greenhouse," Mary suggested. "Let's go, Barkley. Ladies, we need to keep the bloom safe and alive while we continue our investigation. And we should inform the police about our findings, though I doubt Inspector Fletcher will be pleased to hear from us."

Zaclan's cleverness led to the creation of a rose unlike any other, and that very genius might be the reason for his demise.

As soon as they reached the greenhouse, Ponsonby gently took the plant from Mary. "I should keep this in my room, my lady. Then I can ensure this rose receives the care it needs."

"You're right. That would be best. In the meantime, we need to find out more about all of Zaclan's work. Particularly, who might've known about this rose," Mary said, her voice resolute. "There must be records, correspondences, something that can lead us to the truth."

"We'll help, Lady Mary," Margie said, her eyes shining. "Whatever it takes."

Mary smiled. She knew she could always count on these three.

* * * * * 🐾 * * * * *

THE NEXT DAY, Mary headed to the local horticultural society to learn more about Zac's work and his connections. She had hoped to find someone who could shed light on the significance of the unique rose and any potential rivals or admirers Zac might've had.

Accompanied by Ponsonby and Barkley, Mary arrived at the society's headquarters, a charming building nestled amid beautifully maintained gardens. Inside, a knowledgeable and amiable curator greeted them.

"Your Grace," the portly man said warmly, shaking the hand she offered. "What a pleasure it is to meet you at last. Zac has told me so much about you. How can I assist you today?"

Mary explained the situation, careful to omit the more sensitive details of the ongoing investigation. "I recently discovered a remarkable rose in Zaclan's room." She concluded by showing him a drawing of the flower that Margie had drafted. "I was hoping you could tell me more about its significance and whether anyone else knew of its existence."

The curator examined the sketch with great interest, his expression opened with unexpected clarity. "This is extraordinary," he said, his voice filled with admiration. "Mr. Tamberton mentioned working on a new hybrid rose, but I didn't know he'd succeeded so much. This rose could revolutionize the horticultural world."

Mary felt a surge of vindication at his words. "Do you know if anyone else was aware of his progress?" she asked.

Nodding thoughtfully, the curator said, "Tamberton had a few close colleagues and correspondents in the field, but he was very secretive about his most ambitious projects. However, there was one person who showed particular interest in his work—a rival gardener named Horace Honeyman. The two had a bit of a contentious relationship, to say the least. In fact, recently Zaclan had told me they only conversed by letters."

Did Horace Honeyman play a role in Zac's death? This is a lead worth pursuing.

"Thank you, Sir. You've been most helpful."

"Where will we find Mr. Honeyman?" Ponsonby asked as they were being walked to the door.

The curator wrote Honeyman's address on the horticultural society's headed notepaper and wished them a good day.

With a new lead in hand, Mary and her companions went back to the estate, eager to delve deeper into this connection of Zaclan's and the potential motive behind his murder. The discovery of the unique rose had opened up a new avenue of investigation.

11

PETALS OF PERCEPTION

Mary and her assistant sleuths enjoyed a variety of specialty teas and fresh-baked crumpets on the terrace, with Barkley resting underneath the table, catching the crumbs. Unusual for England, today was the second warm day in a row. While they nibbled the unique bread, trying to keep the dripping butter from falling on their clothes, they discussed the case. The discovery of the rose was the principal topic and what they should do to follow up.

Dotty, who'd fallen silent while she puzzled something out, peered at Mary seriously and asked, "But why would your neighbor be creeping around your grounds, Lady Mary?" Her question referred to the earlier sleuthing back at the fence separating Snodsbury from the neighboring estate.

"He's a pushy fellow," Mary replied. "Bought the estate next door years ago, seeking to wedge his way into our society here in this county. Unfortunately for him, many of the local men—my late husband, Roland included—were aware of his criminal activities in London, and that led to his being shunned by the community. I give him credit, however. He hasn't given up. And now that most of the older men have gone . . ." Mary paused, "he's become more pushy than ever."

Her brows furrowed, and Dotty's face remained askew. "Do his intentions seem pushy toward everyone, or just with you?" A slight grin played at the edge of her lips.

Mary hesitated. *Is Dotty seeing something I overlooked in my preoccupation? Is the man thinking of marriage with me? Surely not!*

"I'm not sure, Dotty. I never entertained this thought." Mary took a deep breath. "You think he's been coming around to court me?"

"Maybe, or possibly there's another reason. He was around that morning, and now we know he came again later that day. Was there something about the garden party he desperately needed to know, or perhaps be part of?"

Winnie leaned forward, her eyes square on Dotty. "I don't understand. What sort of thing are you claiming?"

"I wish I knew." Dotty shrugged. "The thought just came to me. I find it strange that he was so persistent that day, despite not being invited and knowing he wasn't welcome."

"Well, of course." Winnie waved her hand and sat back. She then sipped her tea, like a proper lady before setting the cup down silently. "The nouveau riche are like that."

Margie reached for another cake and suggested, "He could've hidden something in the grounds."

Laughing, Mary relaxed into the back of the wrought-iron chair. "Like a weapon or a body, you mean? How could he have done that?" A chill ran down her spine. *He maybe did exactly that while I was away, prior to me returning to life at Snodsbury.*

"Lady Mary?" Winnie gazed at her.

Mary flicked a small crumb from her lap and glanced around at the estate. "After the war, we had no money and couldn't keep up the house and grounds. We lived mainly in London—at the home you came to when we first met, in

London, for your debutante ball. Coming here was too painful for Roland, and with only a housekeeper and gardener for staff, it was impossible for them to have us here."

"Did the nosey neighbor, Quiggly Smythe, live next door then?" Dotty asked Mary.

She nodded. "He bought the estate next door when the previous owners couldn't afford to live there any longer." She paused, thinking. "That would have been about 1940."

Dotty rested her chin in her hands, her focus on the conversation unusually intent.

"*You* never thought of selling?" Margie asked.

Mary shook her head. "No, Roland wouldn't do that. It's been in his family since the 1600s. It broke his heart that we couldn't maintain Snodsbury, but he wouldn't sell it. He always hoped for an heir to recover its fortunes."

"So from 1940 to this year, approximately nineteen years, give or take," Dotty replied, "your neighbor has had the run of your grounds, except for your staff, I mean."

"Well, isn't that something?" Mary chortled. "I doubt the old gardener would have seen or heard him if the man had marched in with a brass band."

"Perhaps there is a skeleton buried here somewhere," Margie said, and fixed them with an unblinking look.

In an unusual moment of clarity, Dotty said, "It may not be a murder weapon or a body. It might be a treasure."

Winnie scoffed and mumbled, "Treasure."

"Well loot, from a robbery, is what I mean." Dotty sat back, scowling.

"She's right," Margie replied. "He could just be a garden variety criminal."

Dotty broke out in peals of laughter, and Mary smiled.

"Not that funny," Winnie said, dismissing the cute joke. "If this was something from a robbery, surely, he would have moved it the moment he heard Lady Mary was returning to live at Snodsbury."

Her red curly hair was frizzy as ever in the summer heat, and Dotty wiped tears from her hazel eyes. "One could say the same if it were a dead body, right?"

Steepling her hands, Mary observed the three young ladies puzzle out the case together without her interruption.

"No." Margie tapped the table, and crumbs flitted across the surface. "A bag or case of loot is quickly and easily carried away. A rotting corpse or skeleton, wouldn't be."

Mary shushed them as one of the new maids came to take away the crockery. Once the woman had left, Mary said, "I think you may have hit upon the answer to my nosey neighbor's persistence, ladies. Good thinking, Dotty. Thank heavens it isn't me he's after. I'm too old to be courted."

The girls giggled.

Winnie said, "What if this has nothing to do with Zaclan's death though? A completely different crime, and this is just a mere coincidence."

"Or," Margie said, her eyes sparkling with excitement, "they're linked. Possibly, Zac uncovered the proverbial 'body' and was blackmailing him?"

Putting a hand up, Winnie objected, "But, Zaclan wouldn't know the neighbor was the culprit. He'd probably think Mary, or her late husband, were the prime suspects."

"True," Margie replied. She took a deep breath and released it. "Very well. What if the neighbor thought Zac was *about* to dig up the body?"

Everyone was silent for a moment.

But that persisted past the point of comfortable silence. Margie's eyes darted back and forth as if she were actually scanning her memories. "Zac said that he was going to extend the rose garden because of the new roses he wanted to showcase."

"Yes." Dotty shot to her feet. "Where the sundial is now, right slap bang in the center of the roses at the far end. The walk through the garden will lead visitors right to the new roses."

Margie stood and set her cloth napkin on the table. "We should get some spades or shovels, and go dig. Now."

"Wait," Mary replied. "If you're right, then whatever is there got Zaclan killed. And if my neighbor is still watching, as I have to assume he is, we'll see him."

"He can't kill all four of us," Margie objected. "Five if Ponsonby is with us."

Barkley barked softly, reminding them he was laying under the table.

"Sorry, Barkley," Margie replied. "Six of us."

Winnie laughed. "Even Inspector Fletcher would realize something was wrong if there were a heap of bodies in your garden."

"I agree with Lady Mary," Dotty said. "Maybe we should have the police investigate."

A chorus of boos from Margie and Winnie nearly drowned out the last words Dotty had said.

Smiling, Mary shook her head. "I'd like to find out if there's something out there, too, but in the end, we have to be sensible. Even Ponsonby couldn't move that sundial. I'll phone Inspector Fletcher and get them started." With that, she excused herself, leaving her assistants in suspense.

She returned minutes later and observed the conversation without interrupting them.

"I hope he's saying no," Winnie said. "Then *we'll* have to dig."

"Lady Mary was right about the sundial though, Ponsonby will need help," Margie remarked.

Winnie nodded. "He can bring the footmen and the under-gardeners to assist."

Dotty shook her head. "I believe we'll need a crane to remove it."

Frowning with disappointment, Winnie said, "Then the body can't be under it. Think about it. If a man can't move it, then Quiggly Smythe couldn't have placed that heavy thing over the burial site."

"You're right, Winnie," Margie replied. "Maybe it's lighter than it looks?"

"Or Quiggly had help. In which case, Ponsonby and another man could move it."

"They'll be here after lunch," Mary finally said, re-entering the room. "He did tell me, 'this better not be a wild goose chase because there's an offense for wasting police time.'"

Margie rolled her eyes and grumbled, "Inspector Fletcher never fails to disappoint."

Dotty glanced around. "If we can't dig it up let's at least inspect the area."

They agreed and quickly left the terrace for the rose garden.

"If we're being watched," Margie said, facing forward but darting her gaze across the lawn and hedges to the upper floor of the house next door, "we shouldn't appear to be too obvious what we are planning."

Following Margie's gaze, Winnie replied, "Maybe we should make ourselves very obvious, and he'll try to make a run for it. Then the police will know for sure it was him."

Dotty strolled ahead of the group, Barkley at her side when she called back, "And then maybe we'd be too dead to enjoy our triumph."

Mary laughed. "That's true. That could be a dangerous action. The police won't arrive for another two hours, and we could all end up buried in the garden by then."

"Then we shall re-enact the tour as if trying to understand

how everything happened," Dotty said. "That should appear harmless enough."

With that mutual agreement, they retraced their steps, following Zac's path, and paused at the same spot, all the while discreetly scanning the ground around the sundial for any signs that might hint at something buried there. Even Barkley seemed to understand their quest because he sniffed at the ground all around the sundial.

"What are we looking for?" Margie asked, as they pretended to be themselves on the tour, fawning over the roses. "If there's a body or loot, it would've been buried years ago. We wouldn't find any sign of that now."

"If Smythe has been back creeping around to see his secret's safe," Dotty replied, "maybe there will be signs of digging."

"Well, there isn't," Winnie scolded. "And that's way too obvious. I don't think this is a good plan. Seems a waste of time to me."

The garden around the sundial was pristine, perfectly groomed, as only Zac knew how to do, and exactly as he had left it.

While facing the girls, a flash of light coming from the neighbor's second-floor windows blinded Mary's eyes.

Keeping her expression unchanged, and herding them onward, Mary whispered, "He's watching us, girls. Act naturally. Don't glance around, just set off walking toward the rose bed where Zac was found."

As they approached, the rose bed remained cordoned off, forcing them to observe it from a distance of five feet. Margie faced Mary and asked quietly, "Did you see him spying on us?"

Mary shook her head. "No, but I saw light reflected from his window. From binoculars or a telescope, I suspect. He's definitely interested in what goes on here in the garden. I hope the police can find whatever we suspect to be hidden here."

12

BENEATH THE SURFACE

Just after lunch, as they'd promised, the police brought a small truck with a winch and hook, that dragged the four-foot sundial away, rather than picking it up, destroying the entire bed of roses and geranium ground cover. Mary groaned at the damage to Zac's immaculate flower bed.

At her side, Barkley growled but remained steadfast.

"Why don't you pick it up and set it down on the lawn instead!" she complained from the patio.

As they couldn't hear her with the distance between them, it was no surprise that they ignored her advice. They began digging, and it didn't take long to unearth a human skeleton about three feet down.

"If your neighbor has been watching this spot since Mr. Tamberton began remodeling the garden," Inspector Fletcher said to Mary while glancing toward Smythe's house, "then I think we have our murderer, and now it'll be for two murders."

"I hope so, Inspector," Mary replied. "I'd like to see Zaclan's killer brought to justice."

"We won't know about this body until the forensic people have examined the bones," Fletcher replied, a keen eye on the fresh crime scene. The area was being cordoned off, and he waved Mary and her group aside. "Unfortunately, we have nothing to hold your neighbor on until then. Maybe not even then, if we can't link the skeletal evidence to him." He pursed his lips. "However, I'll have him followed to ensure that he doesn't escape our net."

"When might we know the results, Inspector?" Mary asked.

"A day or two at the latest," Fletcher replied. "At least for the preliminary results."

"And then?"

"Then we must match their findings to a missing person from the time they estimate someone buried the body," Fletcher said. "I'd guess it occurred at least ten years ago—probably longer."

"Will your first searches for matches be here in Norfolk county?" Mary asked. "If so, I would like to suggest you send the forensic results to Inspector Griffiths in London. My nosey neighbor, Quiggly Smythe"—She nodded her head toward the house they could see through tall silvery-gray beech trees—"came from London and is very interested in what's been happening here in my garden."

Fletcher considered this for a moment. "Normally, I'd never invite outsiders into my crime scene, but what you say makes sense. I'll do it."

"Thank you, Inspector."

"Here in Norfolk, we don't have many missing persons in any year. London, though, will have many, and they may not give the search the priority you would prefer."

Alarmed at this, Mary's brow shot up. She hurried off to phone Chief Inspector Ivor Griffiths, with Barkley following in her wake. She needed the Inspector to enlist everyone in the search once the forensic results arrived.

Her excitement at having found the answer so quickly

caused her to blurt out, "Chief Inspector, I . . ." the moment they put her through to Griffiths.

"Your Grace," Griffiths interjected.

Mary stopped. "My apologies. Hello, Ivor. How are you?" She could almost see Griffiths grinning as he replied.

"Very well, Mary. How are you?"

"Oh, just fine," she answered, flustered. "Now, can we get to the reason I'm phoning you? This isn't a social call."

Griffiths chuckled. "It never is with you."

Through a deep exhale she replied, "Will you please listen?"

Laughing again, he replied, "Yes, I'm listening."

Mary explained about the bones found in her garden and why she was sure it was a London crime.

"We know your neighbor Quiggly Smythe very well up here in the capital," Griffiths said. "He may be a country gentleman out there in Norfolk, but here, he's just another thug."

"Here's your chance to nab him. Find a missing person who fits the forensic results when you get them, and the body will have links to my neighbor. I'm sure of it."

Griffiths' reply wasn't as enthusiastic as Mary had hoped. "The results may match no one on our Missing Persons list, Mary. Even if it does, the fact that Smythe's from London, is your neighbor, and seems interested in the activities of your gardener may not be enough to pursue a case."

Mary sweetened her tone. "But you will put people on it to search the moment you get the forensic report, won't you?"

"If there's enough cause for me to do that, I will. Now, when will you be next in town?"

She smiled, though no one could witness her blush. "The faster your team works to solve the murder, the sooner I can be free to visit London."

"Blackmail is a serious offense, you know. We'll be as quick as we can, and, if there is a London connection, I could visit you out there in darkest Norfolk." His last promise came out like a purr, luring her in.

"Inspector Fletcher wouldn't like that," Mary replied. "He sees himself as the hero in this tale."

"I won't interfere in his case," Griffiths assured her. "Unless I'm asked to, of course. I'll just close out the one that's ours."

｡｡*｡🐾｡*｡*｡*

TWO DAYS LATER, the forensic team provided preliminary results in the time they'd promised Inspector Fletcher. The skeleton, buried about fifteen to twenty years earlier, was that of a man in his thirties, who had good teeth, so not a poor man, and had broken his arm as a child. The break having healed properly, also suggested a person of means.

The following three days were anxious ones for Mary and her sleuthing assistants, as they kept an around-the-clock vigil watching the neighbor. Mary phoned Inspector Fletcher every day since he'd told her the results of the report. Of course, she didn't tell him she'd also phoned Chief Inspector Ivor Griffiths daily as well.

On the fourth day after receiving the forensic report, Fletcher told her the victim wasn't someone who'd gone missing locally, which meant his victim might be from London, and, if so, the police might soon arrest Quiggly Smythe for murder, not just once, but twice. Griffiths was going to do the arresting for the London murder, if that turned out to be the case.

Mary didn't like to leave her estate and phone for any length of time but knew she had to. She'd heard that Horace Honeyman was a reclusive character who rarely left his isolated home unless it was to learn something new about roses. His rose gardens were the talk of the county, and wider, but people could rarely see them, he guarded them so fiercely. A visit from a real live Duchess, however, she felt sure would gain her entrance.

※ ✦ ※ ✦ ※ 🐾 ✦ ※ ✦ ※ ✦

MARY'S CONFIDENCE about being admitted because she was a Duchess took a knock when Ponsonby rang the doorbell, and they waited an age for an answer. Smoke rolled lazily from the tall chimneys and drifted down the roof into the garden, confirming the house's occupancy. Without a breeze to disperse it, the smell of burning wood surrounded the house.

"Applewood, I'd say," Ponsonby replied, noticing Mary's nose twitching. "It has the most pleasant scent of all our woods when burning."

"It's smoking quite a bit," Mary remarked. "Do you think the chimney is on fire, or is he using damp wood?"

"Damp wood," Ponsonby replied, ringing the bell again. The sound of the bell tinkling inside the house told them the doorbell was working.

"Mr. Honeyman doesn't like visitors," Mary suggested.

Ponsonby frowned. "He may be in his garden at the back of the house. I'll investigate." He walked along the front of the house, and, turning the corner, disappeared from Mary's view.

Mary considered returning to the car when the door cracked open, and someone peeked out.

"We don't want any," the owner of the face said, in a high-pitched, nervous voice.

She stepped closer to the door. "Good, because I have nothing to sell. I'm here to see Mr. Honeyman."

"Who shall I say is calling?" the voice replied.

Still unable to decide if the person hiding behind the door was an effeminate man or a gruff woman, Mary replied, "The

Duchess of Snodsbury, and I want to talk to Mr. Honeyman about roses."

The door opened, and a floridly dressed man said, "Roses! Why didn't you say? I know all there is to know about roses."

"Mr. Honeyman, I presume?"

"Yes, yes. That's me. The world's leading authority on roses, Horace Honeyman, at your service, Duchess." He gave a stiff nod of his head, that Mary assumed was a bow, and stepped aside to let her enter.

The house smelled of old books, which were piled high on every surface. Including the floor. Stacks of them. Everywhere. Picking her way between them, Mary followed Honeyman through the house to a conservatory at the back, overlooking a lawn on which Ponsonby stood, frowning.

"My butler, Ponsonby," Mary said, noticing the disapproving look Honeyman cast in his direction.

"He has no business in my garden, my sanctuary."

"We got no answer at the door and thought you may be in your . . ." she hesitated, "sanctuary, and we need to see you urgently about a rose."

Honeyman didn't reply but walked to the French door and opened it, asking Ponsonby to enter.

Mary handled the introductions, but it was obvious from their stiff nods that neither man liked the other.

"I don't like uninvited people among my roses," Honeyman added to his icy greeting.

"Perhaps, then, answer your door," Ponsonby replied, forgetting his butler demeanor entirely.

Honeyman scowled. "I don't like uninvited people coming to my door either."

"Well," Mary said, brightly, "we're here now. I'm sure you know of my gardener, Zac Tamberton. He too loved roses."

Honeyman frowned. "Loved?"

"Zaclan Tamberton was murdered, and we're trying to uncover the reason behind it."

"Then why come to me?" Honeyman cried. "I only know about roses."

We'll be here all day if I don't force the pace. "Because, Mr. Honeyman," Mary began, her tone sharp, "Mr. Tamberton was restoring the rose garden at Snodsbury, my home, and we understand he sent you several letters before he died. We don't know what Zaclan's letters to you said, but we believe they weren't friendly."

"He accused me of trying to purloin one of his plants," Honeyman almost shouted. "I breed my own roses, I've no need to steal other people's."

Mary observed his demeanor, and that only strengthened her belief that Zaclan's accusation was likely true. "Was it the dark rose with the golden-tipped petals you were after?"

"Where is it?" Honeyman demanded. "He stole that from me. It's mine."

Mary shook her head. "You'll have to do better than that, Mr. Honeyman. What did you do to get your hands on it? I assume you have it?" Mary decided a subterfuge may elicit a panicky answer.

"I did nothing," Honeyman responded. "I couldn't. I never leave my house."

"Then it wasn't you that people saw skulking in my shrubs on the day of my garden party?" she countered, taking a stab in the dark at something she'd never considered until this moment.

"Certainly not. I wasn't invited to your garden party. How could I possibly be there?" Honeyman stammered, beads of sweat forming on his brow.

Ponsonby stepped closer to the man. "By climbing the fence

from a neighboring property and creeping through the bushes, perhaps?"

"No, I didn't!" Honeyman cried, almost in tears.

Mary felt sorry for the man. Honeyman's composure was unraveling before their eyes, his agitation growing with every passing second. However, someone murdered Zaclan, and incapacitated the lad prior to attacking him. This miserable creature might be responsible. She silently studied him, and she noticed Ponsonby doing the same.

Honeyman flopped down into the only chair not covered in books and covered his face with his hands. "I only wanted to see the rose garden. I didn't hurt anyone," he mumbled through his fingers.

"Perhaps you didn't intend for it to happen," Mary replied. "But things spiraled out of control. Is that what happened?"

"No! I never even spoke to him!" His anxiety intensified, and Mary hoped that if he continued like this, she might uncover some solid evidence.

"Why not?" Ponsonby asked, standing over the man in a way that made Honeyman flinch.

"All right," Honeyman cried, shrinking away from Ponsonby. "I'll explain. Don't hurt me, please."

He really is a sad excuse for a man, but if making him believe Ponsonby might hurt him is what it'll take to get his story, then so be it.

Ponsonby stepped back, and Honeyman straightened up, looking at Mary, saying, "I wanted a cutting."

"Tell me what happened that day," Mary told him. "From the moment you arrived at my home."

Honeyman nodded, peering at Ponsonby and then back to Mary. "I heard about the garden party and the rose garden. Tamberton taunted me, he'd grown a rose to sweep every award at the Royal Horticultural Show's Chelsea Flower Show next year."

"And you have one you thought would win?" Mary asked, guessing the competition would have existed between them and other rose growers.

He nodded miserably. "Ten years I've been developing Honeyman's Heart, and he tells me he has something to establish him as the greatest rosarian ever. A hybrid so exotic that it will dominate conversation for a century."

"Zaclan wasn't one to 'hide his light under a bushel,' as the saying goes," Mary responded, almost giggling. "But that seems fanciful to me. Obviously, it didn't to you?"

Honeyman shook his head. "He dropped hints whenever we met at the Gardening Club in Snodsbury Village. I thought what he was saying was impossible until he brought in a single petal."

His voice dropped to a low, anguished whisper, and Mary feared he might start crying again, which she didn't want. She needed answers. "So you stole the plant?"

"No!" Honeyman cried. "I just wanted to take a cutting for my garden. I could do a hybridization of my own from that and then I'd become famous as well."

"What happened that day?" Ponsonby demanded.

"I climbed over the wall from your neighbors, like you said." Honeyman pointed at Ponsonby. "I waited at the rose garden until Tamberton came along on his tour to talk about all of his blooms. I thought he'd be so vain he'd point out his unique hybrid to his audience." He paused.

"And?" Mary asked.

"He didn't. He just stood there prattling about the 'depth of the beds' and 'horse manure' and . . ." Honeyman stopped. Then recollected himself. "I was hiding near a tap to a hose. I just snapped and turned it on."

Mary nodded. "You soaked those standing at the front."

Honeyman's eyes darted downward, his shoulders hunched, and a faint flush crept up his neck. His lips pressed into a thin line as if he'd been caught with his hand in the biscuit tin, unable to muster a convincing defense. "I never thought it would work so well. Only, for a second, Tamberton's and my eyes met. I ran."

So that must be what Tamberton went off to take care of. "You ran?"

Honeyman nodded. "Tamberton was a vigorous man, and that intimidated me. I didn't want to face him."

"I can understand that," Ponsonby said, his voice dripping with contempt.

"Thought he'd come right after *me*," Honeyman continued. "But he didn't. The noise and confusion created a distraction, I suppose. When I looked back, he was calming the group, which allowed me to escape."

"You left a glove," Mary said.

Honeyman nodded, unhappily. "I'd taken gloves to protect my hand while taking the cutting. It fell from my pocket when I ran. I noticed only after I got home."

"Why would you not go back to look for it?" Ponsonby asked.

Again, Honeyman shook his head. "I didn't kill Tamberton, I swear it."

"Did you see anyone else hiding among the bushes?" Mary asked.

"No. No one."

"You have to confess this to the police," Mary told him. "This is important evidence."

"I wasn't involved and saw nothing," Honeyman cried. "How could that possibly be important evidence?"

Mary sighed. "Because they know someone entered the garden and suspect that person might be the murderer. If it was you but you aren't the murderer, they need to hear that."

Honeyman groaned and buried his face in his hands again. "I only want to be alone with my roses. I can't face the police. You tell them."

"I will, but that won't save you a visit from them, Mr. Honeyman. You'd best go to them, and tell them what you saw and did."

He nodded without looking up.

Mary signaled Ponsonby they were leaving, and they walked through the narrow path among the books to the front door.

Outside, Ponsonby asked, "Do you believe him, my lady?"

"I'm afraid I do," Mary replied, as she waited for Ponsonby to open the car door. "I can't imagine him confronting Tamberton, and how would he know he had been drugged already?"

"He didn't need to know," Ponsonby said as Mary settled into the back seat of the Rolls, and he took his place at the wheel. "He could have come upon Mr. Tamberton who was already unconscious, face down in the rose bed, and simply pushed his face into the manure."

"It's possible, I suppose," Mary agreed.

"Maybe the police will have some success there," Ponsonby replied, as he drove the car away from Honeyman's house. "They can encourage people to talk in ways that we can't."

WHEN SHE ARRIVED HOME, Mary was delighted to discover all three young sleuths eagerly waiting to hear the news of her meeting with Honeyman. She and Ponsonby were recounting the conversation they'd had when the hall phone rang.

Ponsonby scuttled out to answer it and returned a moment later, with Mary waiting at the drawing room door.

"Chief Inspector Griffiths for you," Ponsonby said, as she pushed past, hustling to the phone.

"Yes, Ivor?" Mary said, the moment she had the handset. "You have a match?"

She listened silently as Griffiths told her what they'd uncovered until he said, "Happy now?"

Mary was more than happy. "Oh, yes," she said. "I think we have our murderer, and I will have a nice new neighbor soon." There was little more to say. She hung up the phone, returning to the drawing room in time to hear Margie ask the others, "What will the phone call say?"

"The Chief Inspector sounded upbeat," Ponsonby replied, not seeing Mary standing quietly in the doorway, a seraphic smile on her face.

Dotty was flitting around, chasing Barkley as he nosed his way around the outer perimeter of the room. "Then we need to find evidence the nosey neighbor killed Zac too."

"I think the evidence we found that led Barkley and the police dog to the fence will be enough," Winnie replied, and Barkley's ears perked up.

Shaking her head, and frizzy hair, Dotty flounced down in a nearby wingback chair. She adjusted her skirt. "I don't. And I particularly want to avenge Zac's death." She peered up at the group, her cheeks rosy.

Mary closed the door behind her noisily. "They have a match, and they have a link to my neighbor," she announced. "Chief Inspector Griffiths will be here tomorrow afternoon."

Barkley grumbled, and Margie rushed to Mary's side. "What exactly did he say?"

The group was on the edge of their seats, even Ponsonby seemed on tiptoes.

"I should let him tell you when he arrives."

"Lady Mary..." the girls began, but Mary's laughter cut their groans off.

"Very well," she said. "The victim, a man called Neland Oliphant, had an addiction to snuff, among other things, including gambling and drugs. He disappeared in 1941, owing some very unpleasant people a substantial amount of money, one of whom was..." She trailed off for dramatic effect, and a sly smile tugged at the corners of her lips as she savored the suspense hanging in the air.

"Mary!?" the three young ladies cried.

"Quiggly Smythe. Who else did you think it would be? The police had even interviewed my neighbor in 1941 about that particular case. He had spent most of his time in London back then, but they found no evidence to suggest foul play."

"They thought Neland Oliphant had fled abroad," Ponsonby said. "I remember that was the talk of the town at the Butlers' Club. Neland's butler claimed it was fishy, but everyone knew what a rackety fellow Neland was. Public opinion—well, the Butlers' Club opinion—favored living abroad under an assumed name. He wouldn't have been the first."

"Does Chief Inspector Griffiths think he can find enough evidence to arrest?" Margie asked.

"He thinks working with Inspector Fletcher they can get a conviction for one or both murders," Mary replied.

"Poor Zac," Dotty murmured, her voice soft with sympathy. "He just wanted to make people happy. He never imagined something would be found that was so terrible."

Winnie shook her head. "It's enough to put me off gardening for good. Who knows what might be buried beneath the soil, when you really think about it?"

"Not necessarily murder victims though," Mary said. "Who is on watch tonight? Our two-time murderer might be getting anxious over the bones being found and ready to run."

"Wouldn't he want to live abroad under an assumed name also?" Margie asked. "It's me tonight, but I hope you'll all be ready if I call for you?"

The others assured her they would be. They'd been keeping watch from one of Snodsbury Hall's garret rooms that faced the neighboring house. From there, they had a clear view of the side of the house with the garages, providing an excellent sightline to both the front and rear of the property. This vantage point served as the perfect observation spot, allowing them to remain indoors and safe.

"He can't know that the police have found a match with links to him, though, can he?" Ponsonby asked Mary.

"I would think not," Mary replied. "After all, the discovery isn't from the local force where he might have spies operating."

"What if he still has spies in the London police?" Dotty asked. "If he's still active there."

"So tonight is the night," Margie said, smiling. "I'm going to catch him." She fidgeted in her seat with anticipation.

"You're going to alert us, and we're going to phone the police, dear," Mary avowed, not wanting Margie creeping downstairs and out to the neighboring house in a foolish act of bravado.

"Of course." Margie sat up straight. "Still, it will be me that spotted him trying to escape. I can see the headlines now..."

Mary called them to order. "We're a team, ladies. It's all for one and one for all with us."

"And I'm D'Artagnan," Margie said, brimming with energy again.

The others groaned. Winnie threw a cushion at her.

"All right, get to your post, and keep the heroics to yourself," Mary chided.

Seemingly undaunted Margie added, "I'm right. I don't know exactly how, but I can feel everything coming together, the London police spy, the murderer's flight, and me, the hero." She giggled and wished them goodnight before setting off.

13

BLOOMS AND ALIBIS

Margie

By four o'clock in the morning, Margie had almost succumbed to exhaustion. The wave of excitement that had sustained her through the dark hours was fading, leaving her eyes gritty, dry, and itchy, with heavy eyelids. Her spirits dipped low. She got up, stretched, and walked around the room, doing anything to stave off sleep, though she knew the neighbor had likely already made his escape.

The sky lightened, and daylight began creeping into the room.

Returning to the window, she saw something that puzzled her. A car sat parked on the main road, almost invisible behind a hedge and trees, between the Snodsbury estate's gatehouse lodge and the driveway to Smythe's house. She stared. *Was that there already, and I missed it? Did it drive up and park while I stretched? Is it the police? That looks like a police car—though it doesn't have a blue light on top. Should I wake Lady Mary?*

Margie scanned the scene outside the window, hoping to see

the constable patrolling the neighbor's gate and boundary. *Where is the police officer on duty? He's not to be seen. Maybe the car is a police car, and he's inside handing over to the next shift?* Margie's panic grew as she wrestled with how she should proceed.

A movement in the bushes beside the car, made the decision for her. She picked up the hand bell they'd made ready for raising the alarm and shook it hard. Its loud clanging echoed from the walls of the room, and she rushed to the door and flung it open so the bell's clamorous notes would reverberate along the corridor and down the stairs. Torn between continuing to ring the bell and getting back to the window to see what happened next, Margie yelled as loud as she could, "He's running!"

She headed back to the window, still ringing the bell, just in time to see the car's lights flicker on as it pulled away from the curb. Dropping the bell, she grabbed the binoculars, desperate to catch the numbers on the car's plate through any gaps in the bushes. But by the time she focused the lenses, the car had already disappeared behind the trees. Seeing Ponsonby and Barkley race down the drive toward the road offered her the only glimmer of hope. Her stomach churned. She'd hesitated when a hero would have acted, and now the villain had escaped.

Running downstairs to the front door, she hoped Ponsonby would return with the car's plate number or description and recover some vestige of value from this awful moment. She found Mary on the hall phone, talking to the local police station.

Placing her hand over the phone, Mary asked, "Which way did they go, Margie?"

"East," Margie said, her voice quavering. "And it was a dark car, like a police car."

Mary relayed this to the police saying, "He'll be heading for the coast. He must have a boat nearby, or know someone who does." Mary nodded and hung up the phone.

"Well done, Margie," Mary cried. "They'll catch him long before he reaches the coast."

Margie almost in tears, mumbled, "I made a mess of it. I watched it happening and couldn't understand what was unfolding. We could have caught him right outside the gate, if I'd woken you quicker."

"Nonsense. You did the right thing by making sure and then raising the alarm. Remember, the police were the ones responsible for watching the house, not us."

Unconsoled, Margie replied, "But we knew. Did they?"

"If they didn't, that isn't our fault either," Mary said. "Now, here's Ponsonby and Barkley. Let's see if they learned anything."

"I have a part of the number," Ponsonby stated. "And the car was a Mercedes."

Nodding, Mary stated, "Phone the sergeant, and tell him. I'll get Margie a medicinal brandy. It's been a shock."

"Very well, my lady." Ponsonby picked up the handset and prepared to dial the number. "Barkley and I will return to the neighbor's house once I've spoken to the police. There was a police constable watching the house when I locked up for the night. I fear he may need help."

Mary led Margie away leaving Ponsonby to relay his new information to the sergeant.

As the color once again blossomed in Margie's face, the two other assistants arrived in the drawing room.

"Why didn't you wake us?" Winnie cried, seeing Margie's condition and Mary in her curlers.

"I rang the bell as loud as I could," Margie protested. "Lady Mary heard. Ponsonby heard. Why didn't you?"

Anxiously flitting to Winnie's side, Dotty asked, "Are you all right?"

She shrugged. "I felt unwell."

"Awake all night?" Mary asked with a concerned half smile.

"Do you need food?" She motioned to the girls, tightening the belt on her robe. "We'll raid the pantry."

As they made their way through the dimly lit hallway, Dotty linked her arm with Margie's.

"We must have nourishment. It's going to be a long day," Mary continued, and they fished out a loaf of bread from the kitchen.

They were eating toast and marmalade when Ponsonby, Barkley, and a pale young man in a police uniform entered the house.

"You look as if you've had a dreadful night, constable," Mary said. "We have hot tea, oodles of sugar, and toast. Eat and drink, it'll help you recover."

The man accepted a cup Dotty quickly handed to him. "Thank you. I've a bump on my head the size of a duck's egg." He gingerly touched the back of his skull, wincing.

"I'll phone the sergeant," Ponsonby said. "And we should have a doctor examine the constable as soon as possible."

"The police doctor will want to do that," the constable noted. "The sergeant will arrange it."

"Very well," Mary said, nodding to Ponsonby. "Be sure the sergeant understands he has an injured man here."

Frowning, Ponsonby's tone was grave. "I don't understand why they aren't here already." But he quickly composed his features.

Just then, the wailing sirens of approaching police vehicles filled the air.

"Perhaps I should step outside," the young constable said, setting down his half-finished cup.

"Not until you've finished your tea," Mary replied.

He did as told, then followed Ponsonby out of the door.

"Now we wait," Mary said to Barkley, holding him back.

"And hope we hear good news in advance of Chief Inspector Griffiths arrival."

CHIEF INSPECTOR GRIFFITHS arrived at Snodsbury by mid-afternoon, explaining that they had caught the neighbor just as he was preparing to board a boat from a nearby estuary. Griffiths and Fletcher then spent two hours interrogating him but made little progress.

"How limited?" Mary demanded to know.

"He denies being responsible for either of the murders," Griffiths told them, stroking Barkley's ears as the group listened eagerly to the story.

"Well, he would, wouldn't he," Mary replied. "But it is him, we know it is."

Griffiths grimaced. "You would think so, and it may prove so." He began slowly, "Only, he has an alibi for the time of Mr. Tamberton's death. He met a group of his past business associates and has several witnesses, some of whom are honest people, to back him up."

The group stared at him in bewilderment. Only Mary spoke. "I don't believe them. You will still get him for the body in my rose garden, though. Won't you?"

"I intend to," Griffiths said. "I don't believe in coincidences of this kind. He buried the body in your garden, I know, and we'll prove it, eventually. The alibi for Mr. Tamberton's murder will be harder to crack."

"Then we're back at the beginning," Margie said. "And we have no other suspects."

"That's Inspector Fletcher's case," Griffiths said. "I can't help you there." As if to avoid further discussion, he bent down and gave his full attention to Barkley who was a favorite with Griffiths, as Griffiths was to Barkley.

"We need time to consider," Mary told the others. "I was so sure that Smythe was the murderer, I'm afraid I lost sight of the other people on our list. We will reconvene for tea at four, and, as Margie says, start again at the beginning."

14

SNUFF, SCANDALS, AND SECRETS

Mary poured herself a cup of Earl Grey, pondering the case. *The neighbor's alibi throws a wrench into our theories, but I refuse to let that deter us. I know the answers are out there, waiting to be uncovered.*

As the clock struck four, everyone gathered in Mary's elegant drawing room. The scent of freshly baked scones and steeping tea filled the air, offering a brief comfort amid the turmoil of the investigation.

"So, where do we stand?" Dotty asked, nibbling on a cucumber sandwich.

"We need to reassess everyone connected to Mr. Tamberton," Mary replied. "We can't afford to overlook anyone."

"Agreed," Ponsonby chimed in, setting down a tray of delicate pastries. "Perhaps we should start with those who had the most to gain from Tamberton's death."

"Horace Honeyman," Margie said through a yawn. "He became Zac's rival and had a vested interest in his work."

"And let's not forget the mysterious new rose," Winnie added, her eyes heavy-lidded and rimmed with a faint shadow of fatigue. "If it's as valuable as we suspect, someone might've killed Zaclan just to get their hands on it."

Mary nodded. "Ponsonby, did you find any of the correspondence between Zaclan and Honeyman? That may give us something more to go on."

"I did, my lady," Ponsonby replied, handing her a bundle of letters. "Like all talented gardeners, Zac kept things he valued in the potting shed. That's where the letters were, and very well hidden too. Zac and Honeyman exchanged quite a few missives, and some of them were heated."

Mary skimmed through the letters, her brow furrowing. "It seems Honeyman had a desperation to outshine Zaclan. He mentions a new project he's working on, something that would 'revolutionize the horticultural world.'"

"That sounds suspicious," Dotty said. "Could Honeyman have stolen Zac's work and killed him to cover it up? Or perhaps, the other way around?"

"Maybe Zaclan isn't the fine, upstanding citizen we all believe him to be." Winnie put her fingers to her pursed lips.

"Interesting," Mary mused. "But we need more concrete evidence either way."

"What about the snuff business?" Margie asked. "We could go back to that theory. Possibly someone wanted Zac out of the way to take over the empire?"

She chuckled. "I'm not sure we can call it an empire. Though, Zaclan's involvement in the snuff trade might've made him some dangerous enemies."

Winnie waved a thin hand. "We never really checked into his personal life. He was quite charismatic. Maybe there's someone who had a more personal motive."

The room fell silent as they considered the possibilities.

Mary coughed as her mind strayed to the young gardener's

charisma. "We need to be thorough. No more wild goose chases. Ponsonby, can you gather more information on Honeyman? And see if you can find any clues about Zaclan's actual involvement in the snuff trade."

"Of course, my lady." Ponsonby bowed.

"Dotty, Margie, and Winnie, can you dig into Zaclan's personal life? Speak to anyone who might have known him well and see if there were any tensions or conflicts."

"Will do," Dotty answered, the other two nodding as well.

"And I'll continue to work with the inspectors."

LATER THAT EVENING, Mary settled into her study, reviewing the letters exchanged between Zaclan and Honeyman. The rivalry between the two men stood out clearly, but beneath it lay something deeper—a hint of desperation in Honeyman's words—that troubled her.

A soft knock at the door interrupted her thoughts. "Come in," she called.

Ponsonby entered, a stack of papers in his hands. "I returned to the potting shed and found more on Honeyman, my lady," he said. "I think Zac had gathered dirt on Honeyman. Maybe he already sensed the direction their rivalry was taking. Anyway, it appears Honeyman has spent all his family money on his obsession and is struggling financially. His comfortable life and his reputation are at stake, and he saw Zac as a direct threat."

Mary's eyes narrowed. "That could be a motive. If Honeyman thought Zaclan's new rose creation would ruin him, he might have been desperate enough to kill."

"Indeed," Ponsonby agreed. "But we need proof. These

papers don't tell us enough, though they're a good place for me to start."

"Yes, we do. So, we don't think there's anything to Zaclan's character that is 'not up to snuff' as one might say?"

Ponsonby chortled. "Clever, my lady. Not that I can derive from anything I've seen, heard, or found. However, Zac wouldn't likely keep incriminating items somewhere easily found. We might try a bank safe deposit box, perhaps."

"Good idea. And we need to go deeper into the snuff business." She tapped the letter on her desktop. "There's more to this than just a horticultural rivalry."

"We'll find the answers, my lady."

Mary nodded. "I know we will. Thank you, Ponsonby."

As Ponsonby left the room, Mary reclaimed her seat at her desk, her mind tossing around the possibilities. The pieces of the puzzle were slowly coming together, but the picture was far from complete.

After an unsatisfactory hour of solitary contemplation, Mary phoned the police station and asked for Chief Inspector Griffiths. When he came to the phone, Mary started the usual polite conversation before asking, "Have you charged my neighbor, Quiggly?"

She guessed by his hesitation that he hadn't. "Not yet. We need to find more evidence to link him to the bones. We've released him for now."

"Won't he attempt to escape again?" Mary cried.

"I hope so," Griffiths replied. "That way the judge might block bail. His story about heading to Europe for business and pleasure, rather than attempting to escape justice, sounded too convincing."

Mary pressed him, her curiosity piqued. "How did he explain your constable being knocked unconscious?"

"He says that happened entirely coincidentally—a burglar

burgled his house that night. He hadn't noticed this because his early start had left him no time. It was the mysterious burglar who assaulted the constable, not him."

She shook her head. "I don't believe it! And I can't believe any judge would either."

"Can you prove it didn't happen, though," Griffiths asked. "We couldn't, so that's that. Another escape attempt would be welcome, in my mind."

Crossing her arms in an act of defiance that no one could see, Mary asked, "You think when there are two unconscious constables it will be enough to convince the local idiot judge?"

"Our surveillance will be more awake, this time," Griffiths said, his laughter crackling through the phone line.

"What if he tried to damage the crime scene?" Mary's tone shifted to one of caution. "He may know there's still something buried out there that you haven't found yet. He may want to find and remove it."

"We dug in a wide area around the grave," he replied. "Deeper than the buried remains even. I can't believe there's anything left to find there."

"Probably not," Mary admitted, frowning. "But I still think something like that is a possibility."

"The local force isn't big enough to watch him and your garden, Mary," Griffiths replied. "I wish it were so, but it isn't. Get those three assistants of yours to watch, but only from the house, mind. No wandering out in the grounds alone until we have both murderers in custody."

Mary assured him she wouldn't let her assistants get into danger, and they ended the call.

"It seems the police are doing as badly as we are," she murmured to herself, stroking the dog's head.

Barkley sighed, and yawned, having done his part in bringing Quiggly Smythe to justice.

"Come, Barkley," Mary urged, and the dog swaggered forward at a snail's pace. "We'll let the girls know they're back on night shifts as of this evening. They'll be pleased. They like having something to do." A shadow of doubt flickered through her mind, shaking her optimism. *Can I really protect them from the dangers of the world?*

15

THE SCENT OF TROUBLE

When Mary stepped outside the following morning, the sun cast a golden glow over Snodsbury, illuminating the dew-kissed petals of Mary's prized roses. Birds chirped merrily, and the world around her seemed at peace. Yet, an undercurrent of unease rippled through Mary as she made her way to the garden for a morning walk.

The dog trotted beside her, his stubby tail wagging and his nose sniffing the air. Not even her beloved corgi could comfort her today.

As Mary rounded the corner to the section of garden left unmarred by crime-scene tape and police feet treading down every surface, her eyes landed on a figure sprawled among the vibrant blooms. Her heart skipped. *Not again!*

Barkley reached the body first, barking urgently. Mary's breath caught in her throat as she recognized the lifeless form of her unpleasant neighbor, Quiggly—his face twisted in an expression of shock and fear, similar to Zac's.

"Ponsonby!" she shrieked most unladylike, her voice sharp. Within moments, her loyal butler appeared at her side.

"Good heavens," he muttered, his usually composed servant demeanor faltering. "Not again!"

"That's what I just said." She threw her hands up. "All right. Quick, we must alert the authorities. And seal off the garden. No one must disturb the scene."

Ponsonby nodded, hurrying off to make the arrangements. Mary knelt beside the body, careful not to touch anything. Barkley whined, nudging her gently as if to offer comfort. *Pretty soon my entire garden will be cordoned off.*

INSPECTOR FLETCHER ARRIVED WITH A TEAM, the mood somber as they surveyed the scene. Fletcher's eyes narrowed as he approached Mary.

"This is becoming a habit, Duchess," he said, his tone accusatory.

Mary bristled, but kept her composure. "Believe me, Inspector, I take no pleasure in finding dead bodies in my garden. Mr. Smythe posed a constant annoyance, but I would never wish him harm."

"Convenient that your enemies keep pushing up the daisies," Fletcher said with a wry smile that Mary did not return. "It seems we need to question your household again, and perhaps more thoroughly this time."

How dare he. Mary's jaw tightened. "My neighbor wasn't my enemy, and as I mentioned, Mr. Smythe annoyed me, but nothing more. We'll cooperate fully. But, none of my guests or my staff are responsible. Nor am I!"

"I'll see about that," Fletcher said, turning to address his team. "Secure the area, and begin a thorough investigation. I want every inch of this garden searched."

As the police combed the garden for clues, Mary gathered her friends in the drawing room. Dotty, Margie, and Winnie appeared shaken, their earlier enthusiasm for sleuthing now dampened by another grim discovery. Even Barkley was exceptionally docile.

Wringing her hands, Dotty said, "This is terrible. First Zac, and now Quiggly Smythe. What if one of us is next?"

Mary cocked her head, flashing a reassuring smile. "Stay calm. We've dealt with challenging situations before, and we'll get through this one too by focusing on finding the connection between these murders."

"Do you think it's all related to Zac's new rose?" Margie asked. "Maybe Mr. Smythe's murder resulted from finding it, thus both men were killed for the same reason."

"It's possible, though it seems unlikely," Mary replied thoughtfully. "We need to find out more about this rose. And also more about my neighbor."

Winnie added, "And we should continue digging into the snuff business. There's more to that story. I'm sure of it."

"Agreed," Mary said.

Dotty pushed past the other two girls. "We can search Zac's room again. We must've missed something."

The group made their way to the room that had been assigned to Zac on the upper floor, as befitted a titled, if penniless man, however, away from both family and regular guest rooms as befitted a working gardener. Mary's heart ached as she peered around, imagining the life Zac had led here, even if only briefly, while completing the garden restorations.

"I'll start with his desk," Mary said, moving toward the cluttered surface. "There may be papers or notes that can give us a clue."

Ponsonby and the girls began sifting through the room, carefully examining every item. Barkley, ever curious, sniffed around, his nose leading him to a small drawer in a night table that appeared to have been overlooked, at least by them. Mary pulled the drawer open, unsure of what she expected to find. It lay completely empty. But Barkley continued to scratch around, barking and sniffing at the bedside table. Mary felt around inside the drawer.

"There's something here," Mary said, as she tugged at a folded piece of paper wedged toward the back, as though it had slipped behind the drawer unnoticed.

She opened it, revealing detailed notes on the cultivation of the new rose variety. Her eyes widened as she read the description, summarizing it for the others. "Zac's rose is unlike any other. It's a unique hybrid, potentially worth a fortune."

"Someone indeed killed Zac for this," Dotty said.

"It seems likely," Mary replied. "But we need to be sure. We must find out who else knew about this rose and had a motive to kill for it."

As they continued their search, Mary's resolve hardened. The stakes ran higher than she had imagined, and she vowed to uncover the truth no matter the cost. The safety of her home and her friends depended on it.

Inspector Fletcher had launched his investigation by the time Mary and her team, including Barkley, returned to the garden. The police officers' meticulously combing through the flower beds filled her with a mix of hope and dread.

"We need to speak with anyone who had contact with Zaclan and Mr. Smythe," Mary said, approaching Fletcher. "There must be someone who can give us a lead."

Fletcher's eyes glinted with suspicion. "You're awfully eager to involve yourself in this investigation, Duchess."

"I care about my friends and my home," Mary retorted. "I want to see justice done."

"Very well," Fletcher said, his tone begrudgingly cooperative.

"We'll start with your remaining guests. But make no mistake, Duchess, I'll be watching you closely."

Mary met his gaze with steely determination. "Do what you must, Inspector. I have nothing to hide." *And you'll be lucky when this is over if you still have a job.*

As the questioning started, Mary's mind raced with possibilities. The game was afoot, and she wouldn't rest until the truth emerged.

"We'll find the answers," she whispered to herself. "We have to."

16

A SPLIT STEM

With the garden once again closed to them, five of the members of the intrepid Society of Six congregated outside—Margie, Winnie, Dotty, Ponsonby, and Mary, with Barkley by her side. Only Cook was missing, working in the kitchen preparing lunch. The terrace, shaded by a large, wisteria-covered pergola, provided a vantage point where they could observe the police at work in the garden below. The vibrant colors of Mary's prized roses stood in stark contrast to the somber mood that hung over the group.

"This is a dreadful business," Dotty said. "First Zac, and now Mr. Smythe. What could connect them?"

Margie tapped her finger on her lips, as her thin eyebrow arched and her green eyes grew dark. "He must've been Zac's killer and the murderer of the body we found. Nothing else makes sense." A chorus of nods and soft affirmations followed her statement.

"That would be the simplest solution," Mary said. "However, Chief Inspector Griffiths is an experienced officer, and he's fairly sure that my nosey neighbor didn't kill Zaclan. He may still be the one who disposed of the body that was dug up in the rose garden, of course. And being murdered himself doesn't make him innocent of any crimes."

Ponsonby coughed discreetly, catching Mary's eye.

Barkley sneezed a fly off his nose, and Mary grinned. Composing her face, she addressed her trusted butler. "Yes?"

"Ma'am, Mr. Smythe's death strongly indicates he murdered the body buried in the rose garden. Perhaps someone has suspected all along that he was a murderer, but without a body, no proof of murder existed."

Mary nodded. "The 'someone-who-suspected' must have had a close relationship with the victim: a brother, a son, a father, or a lover, maybe?"

"Precisely, ma'am," Ponsonby replied. "Now that we know the remains belong to Neland Oliphant, we might find who loved him and that way discover Smythe's murderer."

There was a moment of quiet as the group considered this. Barkley rolled around on the patio blocks distastefully, and Winnie sneered. "I don't care as much who killed the nosey neighbor. It's Zaclan's murderer I want to see brought to justice."

Mary glowered. "We take satisfaction in Mr. Smythe's death, but it's hard not to feel some relief that he's gone, especially if he caused the death of the man buried in the rose garden."

"Then," Dotty said, "our focus must be on Zac's murder—Mr. Smythe's death isn't relevant."

How true is that? Mary considered.

Winnie snapped her fingers and Barkley halted his pursuit of whatever he was rolling in, then trotted to her side and sat obediently. She snickered at him but didn't oblige with a pat. "It's possible they're linked, and there's a motive we haven't discovered, or we haven't found the full extent of everything that connects the crimes."

Her statement led to a short period of quiet thought as Mary mulled over the possibilities. Ponsonby watched the police forensic team like a hawk, and the girls nibbled the sandwiches and cakes that Cook had thoughtfully set out for their lunch.

"What if Zac and Quiggly had become business partners?" Ponsonby suggested. "And Horace Honeyman learned of this. He could've killed Zac to get the rose, and, when he didn't find it, watched Smythe, thinking he might know where to find it."

"And then," Mary said, taking up the thought, "when he or she saw Quiggly standing at a rose bush, assumed it to be the rose and then killed him, only to learn it wasn't after all."

Ponsonby nodded. "Something like that."

"That doesn't work." Winnie shook her head. "Honeyman is an expert on roses. He would've known at a glance that the two men had not been standing beside any new variety of rose."

"Clever thinking. This may not be it, Winnie," Mary replied. "Perhaps just an example, that might lead us to something we haven't thought of yet."

Dotty stared past Mary at something unknown, yet she spoke to her directly. "Still, if that were a valid theory, it would have to be related to where they were standing. Why else would someone kill them both in the garden?"

Margie combed her fingers through her thick honeysuckle hair. "I believe the most likely explanation remains that the two murders aren't related at all. Zac died for something he was doing at that moment, while Quiggly Smythe finally faced death for the murder of the skeleton in the rose garden."

Silence reigned so long, Mary found herself obliged to bring them back to the case. "For now, let's focus on Zaclan's murder while the police investigate Quiggly Smythe's death. We found Horace Honeyman quickly enough, and I met the SNUF Society. Can we refocus on Zaclan's personal life?"

"Margie, Dotty, and I can work on that. I already know one person we can talk to," Winnie said.

"Will they point you in the right direction or to others, though, Winnie?" Mary asked.

Dotty chimed in, her gaze back to the group. "If not, Ursula in the kitchen might. She hasn't stopped crying since we found Zac dead."

"Oh? And I didn't notice that?" Margie quipped, picking at her fingernails.

"You're so busy," Dotty replied with air quotes. "You don't see or hear anything!"

"And you're so dreamy, Dotty, we assume you're clueless," Margie spoke with a twinge of anger.

"Ladies," Mary chided.

Dotty smiled, seemingly unfazed by Margie's slight. "But when I get hungry, I spend time in the kitchen—it's useful to be around the kitchen staff."

Margie stuck out her tongue.

"No one suspected anything between Ursula and Zac because he's a gentleman's son, and Ursula isn't a gentlewoman of any sort," Dotty said, taming her wild curls as the breeze picked up.

"Though she's a pretty, good-hearted girl," Ponsonby chimed.

"Just because she's upset doesn't mean she had an affair with Zac," Margie said, still unhappy at being dismissed as inattentive. "She may have been in love with him, and he might not even have known of it."

"That's true," Mary said. "Ursula is at that impressionable age. Still, Dotty's point is good. We must question Ursula, and you girls may well be best for that. I'll be seen as the heavy-handed Duchess, Ponsonby as a dirty old man, and the police would be a disaster."

"I could speak to her, milady," Cook, who was just arriving with more cakes, cried.

"I fear you're her authority figure in the kitchen, Cook," Mary replied. "It would be best for all of us if you remained neutral and able to reassure her afterward."

Cook's mutinous intensity suggested she didn't quite agree with her mistress's order, but she said, "Very well, Your Grace." Letting Mary know by her formality she was most offended.

"I have a suggestion of my own, my lady," Ponsonby interjected quickly to ward off any further awkwardness. When Mary gestured her permission to him, he said, "Honeyman has a butler. An odd sort of fellow, but he is a member of the Butlers' Club. I ascertained this information when we first learned of his involvement. Maybe I can further our knowledge from him."

"Thank you, Ponsonby," Mary replied. "Learning more about Mr. Honeyman will be invaluable."

Not to be outdone, Cook said, "I could do the same for that nosey neighbor, ma'am. I meet his cook often when shopping in town."

"That too would be of great value. Thank you, Cook," Mary said, beaming. "Once again, we're on the move."

Margie asked, "What will you do?"

Mary laughed. "I shan't be idle. By the way, Ponsonby, would the Butlers' Club furnish us with information on my esteemed London garden party guests?"

Ponsonby assured her it could.

"Then widen your inquiries to include Sir Jolyon and Lord Abernoothy," Mary told him. "They had harsh words about Quiggly that day, which meant nothing at the time but now seems suspicious. Did they know the man? If so, in what capacity? An acquaintance about town or a man to whom they owed money, perhaps?"

"Very well, my lady," Ponsonby replied.

"You still haven't said what you're going to do," Dotty reminded Mary.

"I'm going to phone my London friends and acquaintances and gently quiz them about Zaclan's love affairs, if he had any, and also discover what people know about the SNUF Society. I can't believe they're all as dotty, begging your pardon, Dotty, or as innocent as they appeared when I attended their meeting."

Dotty smiled at her friend's apology and asked, "Why don't you think they are?"

Mary frowned. "They knew I was coming and why, which meant they behaved themselves. I expected that. What made me suspicious was how each member sidled up to me that evening, insisting that the world of snuff had died and nothing could revive it. I felt it odd then, and now, I think it even more so. Had Zaclan blended a new snuff that would take the world by storm and they would all profit from it?"

"Drugs!" Margie cried. Everyone stared at her in surprise. "What if Zac had blended drugs into snuff and they're planning to market them?"

"Some people do sniff drugs," Mary said, thoughtfully. "I wonder if what you say is possible? Chief Inspector Griffiths would know. Let's ask him." She rushed from the terrace to the phone.

17

CHIEF INSPECTIONS

Time dragged on as Mary waited for Chief Inspector Griffiths to be located and connected to the phone. Her excitement began to fade, but it flared again when she finally heard his voice. She quickly explained her call and asked if sniffing snuff and heroin together would work to give people the thrill they crave.

"I've never heard of it being done," Griffiths replied. "But I don't see why not. I'll ask our medical people for their opinion. You think this may be what's behind Tamberton's death?"

"It's a thought," Mary said. "On its own, snuff is a dead business, I'm told. What if Zaclan had concocted a blend that disguised the heroin so well, it could be sold with no one being the wiser?"

"The first person to die of it would give the game away. The heroin would show up in their post-mortem."

"Eventually," Mary agreed. "But maybe it could be years before anyone dies? After all, snuff isn't something the average drug addict buys. If the sales were only among the wealthier members of society, it could go on for years. Think of the profits."

"Wealthy people also die from overdoses," Griffiths said. "Particularly those in the entertainment industries, but I take your point. If the snuff was sold exclusively to respectable individuals, such as through the SNUF Society, it might avoid attracting attention long enough for some people to amass significant wealth."

"You will let us know as soon as you hear?" Mary asked.

"I will," Griffiths replied. "Now, when will I have the pleasure of your company for dinner? I'm here in Norfolk, and you're here in Norfolk, it seems to me we should celebrate that."

Mary laughed. "It's true, we're rarely in the same spot together. Perhaps tomorrow night?"

With that agreement in place and the time settled, Mary hung up and headed back to the terrace, where the discussion now centered on Ponsonby and the Butlers' Club.

Catching on to the conversation as she approached the group, Mary said, "You must go to London and meet them as soon as you've gathered the relevant butlers, Ponsonby. We've talked about it often enough, now you must do it. There's no time to lose."

"Quite so, Your Grace," Ponsonby replied.

Mary reddened. "Sorry, Ponsonby. That sounded like you not meeting the Butlers' Club yet was your fault. We've been too busy, I know, and you more than most."

Ponsonby unbent enough to say he was sure 'her ladyship' had not meant to be anything but eager for him to be off, before asking, "And what did you learn from Chief Inspector Griffiths?"

"He's never heard that a blend of snuff and heroin happened in a case but will ask the police doctors if it could be done," Mary told them. "Now, what are your plans for interviewing the new people we identified, girls?"

When the group had finished debating how they were to carry out their investigations, Mary suggested they start immediately. Her assistants left, chattering about who they should start with. Cook left to begin the next meal and see what she could get out of Ursula prior to the three girls arriving in the kitchen, while Ponsonby went to telephone the Butlers' Club and other butlers he knew.

"What do you say, Barkley?" Mary asked her corgi companion when the others were out of hearing. "You and I will wait for Ponsonby to get off the phone, then I'll contact everyone I know. Someone will know if Zac Tamberton has been sneaking around behind the backs of husbands and fiancés, or even outside the gaze of young women's watchful fathers."

Mary and Barkley entered the house to find the hall was quiet, and the phone was free. Ponsonby, presumably, had finished his arrangements with the butlers. There were, however, raised voices coming from the kitchen. It sounded like her three assistants and Cook hotly debating, with someone wailing piteously in the background. Mary smiled and then meandered upstairs, with Barkley at her heels, to begin her own round of phone calls from her room.

An hour later, after many frustrating repeat calls to friends who were out, she felt she had a reasonable understanding of just how popular the young gardener had been. His family's descent into poverty hadn't dimmed his attractiveness to many of London Society's young women. Mary thought it possible Zaclan could've recovered his own fortunes just by marrying one of the heiress's names she'd been given and wondered if anxious families might have stepped in to prevent that. Could one of the young women be so lost in love that her father saw murder as his best chance to prevent her from throwing herself away on a mere gardener, regardless of his title?

She studied the list of names she'd made and re-read the notes against each. Where to start? She could organize the list by wealth, if Zaclan was trying to recover his fortune, or by the likelihood of success with the girl's family, if he was only interested in his standing in Society. Other ways of organizing it might occur when she'd spoken to the women themselves.

Some names were of girls who'd been in the classes she'd managed for the debutante ball. She felt confident of gaining an audience from them, so she began there. They were eager to help, having heard of Zac's murder, but could shed little light on Zac at all. He'd escorted all of them to one or two functions and been the perfect gentleman in every case. All rather disappointing, was the general feeling Mary gained from the discussions. Nor could they relay any interesting gossip about Zac and other young women. Mary thought: an interest in books, plants, especially roses, and snuff suggested a man who had little interest in carnal matters.

She persevered, and by the end of a second hour had heard enough to decide Zac's murder had little to do with romantic liaisons of any kind as far as she could tell, and she headed outside. This realization was a relief in a way. Unless Zac's romantic fancies ran only with serving girls, one line of enquiry was gone.

This last idea firmly squashed when her three assistants joined Mary on the terrace, roundly complaining about Cook's interference in relation to Ursula, before explaining that Ursula loved Zac because he'd been kind to her whenever they met, 'unlike some people she could mention but wouldn't.' Mary assumed Cook's robust personality was overpowering for a shy girl like Ursula.

"It doesn't seem right," Dotty complained. "A handsome man like Zac not being interested in women."

Margie began hesitantly, "You don't think . . . ?" She trailed off, unable to finish the question.

"He seemed to be friendly with Sir Jolyon," Winnie said.

"That was just their common interest in snuff," Mary replied confidently, though she too had been harboring these disquieting thoughts. Was there a hidden side to Zaclan none of them had known about?

"Maybe Ponsonby will shed some light on this during his investigations among the butlers," Margie suggested.

"I hope so," Mary said. "I'd like to close this line of enquiry if we can. I hate peering into other people's private lives as much as I'd hate others seeing into mine."

"I still favor my brilliant idea about snuff and heroin," Margie said. "So I'm happy to learn more about that and not have to pry into Zac's love life."

"Until we hear from Chief Inspector Griffiths, there's no point," Winnie retorted.

"The police doctor will be just a regular doctor I assume," Margie said.

Ponsonby returned to the terrace. "I shall take the afternoon train to London, ma'am. Is there anything you need in town while I'm there?"

"Will Sir Jolyon's butler be at the Butlers' Club?" Mary asked, after a moment's thought.

"He will," Ponsonby replied, his countenance serious.

"Then when you meet, ask if he knows anything more about the SNUF Society than I got when I was there," Mary said. "Particularly if he mentions Zaclan. He will probably know Mr. Tamberton is dead."

Ponsonby adjusted his cufflinks, a distant gaze aimed toward the window, clearly weighing his words carefully. "It will be a difficult conversation to have. We're like priests when it comes to the personal details of the people we support. Such matters require secrecy akin to the Confessional."

"I'm pleased to hear it, and I understand," Mary replied, smiling. "And we certainly don't want to know anything personal. All we need to know is if Sir Jolyon and Zaclan were closely involved, working together, perhaps, on snuff recipes."

Her butler nodded. "Then if you'll excuse me, ma'am, I'll pack and be off to the station."

Once he left, Margie said, "I'll go phone my father. I think my idea is so brilliant that I feel it in my insides—it's the answer."

"If it is," Dotty replied, "then someone supplied Zac with the heroin. Who might know who that would be? Not one of your social friends, Lady Mary, I'd guess."

Mary agreed, saying, "And yet, there were people I knew that were taking drugs in the old days. It's possible one of them has continued and has become currently involved in bringing them into the country."

Winnie laughed. "I don't see old Lord or Lady Abernoothy as a pair of drug fiends."

Mary remembered both of the Abernoothys as young people in the 'Roaring or Golden '20s' and the 'Dirty '30s' and couldn't rule them out in her mind. The same held true for at least one other couple who'd attended the garden party that day. If Margie's idea proved sound, they needed to find a dealer who knew Zac and was also present that day, giving them two possibilities to start their investigation. She could only hope the theory wasn't feasible.

Margie was already inside by the time Mary's thoughts had drifted into the past. Her smile concealed the growing tension in her chest. They couldn't know how much this was weighing on her. *Could Dotty be right? If there's another body hidden in my garden, what else has gone unnoticed all these years?* "What are our next lines of investigation?"

Winnie nodded. "I want to dig deeper than just his love life."

"Your friend knew him well?" Mary asked.

"When Zaclan's titled family ran into difficulties, they were neighbors," Winnie said. "Caro has known him since he was a boy," Winnie said. "There was even talk of them getting married at one time, but all that ended when Zaclan's father lost everything."

"Dotty?" Mary asked.

"As I said earlier," Dotty replied, "the answer may lie in the location. Both men were killed in the garden and so near to each other, there may be another secret buried there."

"You plan to take out a spade when the police have gone and dig up my roses?" Mary asked, smiling. *I can't let them see how much this is bothering me.*

18

A NEW BLOSSOM

Mary sat at the head of the long mahogany table in the breakfast room, her cup of Scottish breakfast tea forgotten beside her as her mind churned with the fresh information that had surfaced. Abernoothy, once a close friend of her late husband, now stood as a figure of intense scrutiny in their case.

Gazing around at the faces, each waiting to hear what she'd learned, Mary straightened in her chair. "Lord Abernoothy may be more involved in this than we initially thought."

Her assistants said nothing.

"I've had a call this morning from an old friend at the Palace, who told me that Lord Abernoothy had taken a young man under his wing in the late '30s. Abernoothy cared for him like a son, and the man, whose family were all overseas, vanished in the early '40s."

"And you think this young man could be the skeleton we found?" Dotty asked as a spark of realization lit her gaze.

Mary nodded. "I'm afraid I do. Abernoothy may have suspected that Quiggly Smythe—who we know had a questionable past—was responsible for the young man's death. It's possible that Abernoothy has been harboring a grudge all these years. When Smythe moved out of London and next door to me, Abernoothy may have suspected the man buried the body here in Norfolk, well away from London, where, if it had been discovered, might have connected the crime back to him."

Margie interjected, "Then when the bones surfaced, Lord Abernoothy immediately jumped to the conclusion they belonged to his young friend from all those years ago?"

"Who else could it be? Quiggly Smythe and the skeleton of a young man all in the same small neighborhood is too much of a coincidence. When Abernoothy heard the estimated time of the victim's death, it certainly consumed him, and he came here for revenge."

"But he didn't stay here at Snodsbury after the police interviews, Lady Mary," Dotty reminded her. "He'd left by the time of Mr. Smythe's death."

"I suspect he stayed somewhere nearby," Mary said. "And waited." She paused. "Or he contacted Smythe and asked to meet."

"They met right where they found the skeleton?" Margie asked. "Would they do that?"

"I don't know," Mary admitted. "But they did. And Abernoothy took his revenge, so long in the making."

"If Abernoothy killed Smythe, then we need to figure out how Abernoothy knew it was Smythe."

"He may have been told in the '40s, I mean, that Quiggly was responsible for his friend's death but not given proof. Then waited, hoping eventually his friend's body would be found, and an investigation begun. He might've kept a close eye on Mr. Smythe, waiting for that time so when it came, there'd be an opportunity."

Mary's eyes narrowed with the thought of the long bitter wait Abernoothy had endured. "And that opportunity came when Zaclan began digging up the old rose garden," Mary continued. "Abernoothy waited a long time for the crime to be uncovered and to get his justice."

"It's all good timing," Margie murmured. "Maybe too good. We don't have any proof of this."

Dotty absently played with a muffin crumb and muttered, "Too good. Would anyone kill someone for a crime committed nearly twenty years ago?"

Mary's gaze shifted to the window, where the morning light filtered through the sheer curtains. The room fell silent. Pieces of the puzzle were coming together, but the picture they formed was still murky.

"Why would Lord Abernoothy kill Zac though?" Margie asked, cocking her head. She tilted her head slightly as if trying to pull together an impossible case. Her lips parted, then closed again, as if she would say more, but didn't, the confusion clear in her wide eyes as she absentmindedly twisted a strand of her hair.

"I still think Quiggly Smythe killed Zac, I just don't know why," Mary replied.

"Then Abernoothy is our prime suspect," Winnie stated. "For at least Smythe's murder. He had the motive, the opportunity, and, if he was really close by, the means to carry out the crime."

"We may never know why Smythe killed Zaclan. But we need more than just speculation about why he killed the body in my rose bed," Mary replied.

The sound of footsteps echoed in the hallway, and Ponsonby appeared at the door. "My lady, there's a telephone call for you. It's the inspector."

Mary rose from her seat, her heart pounding in her chest. "Thank you. I'll take it in the study." *I might as well discuss Abernoothy with him as well.*

As she walked to the study, her mind raced with the implications of her next move. Abernoothy, a man she had known for many years, now surfaced as the prime suspect.

She picked up the receiver, her voice steady despite the turmoil inside her. "Inspector Fletcher."

"Duchess," the inspector's voice crackled through the line. "I've been reviewing the evidence you provided concerning the new rose, and I believe we need to speak further."

"Inspector, I now have reason to believe that Lord Abernoothy may be involved in the murder of my neighbor."

A brief pause lingered on the other end of the line. "Abernoothy? Are you certain?"

"As certain as I can be. Without concrete evidence."

"Mm-hmm."

"Inspector, I understand your hesitation, but I said I'd give you anything I learned, and I believe the motive we've discovered is strong enough to warrant further investigation. Abernoothy had a deep connection to the skele—I mean the young man, Neland Oliphant. He might have believed, or even been told, that Smythe was guilty of Oliphant's death. Only without the body, he hadn't enough certainty to exact revenge on Smythe. But when the bones surfaced so close to Smythe's house, he knew and acted."

"I'll get the team to investigate Abernoothy. If he's involved, we'll find out, but this is really just hearsay and speculation, you know. You're not providing evidence or proof of anything."

Mary sighed with relief. "Thank you, Inspector. I know it's just a theory and hope you'll be discreet until we have something concrete."

"Don't worry, Duchess," Fletcher replied. "Unlike you, I'm a professional. It's not my job to destroy innocent people. However, if there is anything in what you suggest, we'll find it."

Mary hung up the phone, her heart still racing. *I'm not sure if*

I am reassured by that or not? She circled back to the group in the breakfast room.

"I've informed the inspector of our theory," she said, her voice steady. "They're going to investigate Abernoothy. If he's responsible, we'll know soon enough."

"You need to tell Chief Inspector Griffiths the same information," Winnie said. "After all, he may not have connections in such high places as the Palace and not know any of this."

"You're right, Winnie," Mary replied, promptly returning to the phone in her study and dialing the local number Ivor Griffiths had given her.

"This is just old gossip, Mary," Griffiths said, when she recounted what she'd been told.

"Gossip is usually correct, in some fashion, Ivor," Mary replied. "People hear and see things. They may not always understand it well, but there's truth in it somewhere."

He laughed. "You read too much Agatha Christie, but I will follow up on this. Someone in Abernoothy's circle will know more. If there's truth in it, then it's a powerful motive for Inspector Fletcher's case. I hope you've told him?"

"I have," Mary replied, rather cross he thought she was so slow-witted. "And now I'm telling you because it may be important to your case."

"It might help us finally confirm the dead man's identity," Griffiths agreed. "We have a good idea, but there's so little left, and the bones have so few distinguishing features, we wouldn't have a suitable case against anyone."

"Are you really hoping to make a case against anyone alive today?" Mary asked.

"This was murder, and if the murderer is alive, then yes, I hope to bring the villain to trial," Griffiths replied. "However, I'm not very hopeful, if I'm honest. I have murders happening today that occupy most of my time. Our poor young Neland may never have justice."

"I fear Lord Abernoothy may have taken vengeance into his own hands," Mary said. "If he has, I can only hope that he was correct in his assumption."

"There's no reason he would've killed your gardener, Zac, though," Griffiths countered. "I think that has to be your neighbor, and the only reason he'd do that, that I can think of, is he knew of the skeleton and killed Zac to stop further digging."

"I agree," Mary replied. "That gives me some comfort. If my old friend Abernoothy killed Smythe in error, then he at least killed someone who deserved retribution."

Griffiths laughed. "The law won't agree that's a good enough reason, I'm afraid."

"Zaclan was a wonderful young man, and he didn't deserve what happened to him," Mary said. "Sometimes the law really is a fool."

"Well, this branch of the law will try not to be too foolish," Griffiths replied, still amused. "I'll keep you informed of our progress. Now, about our dinner date?"

Mary hesitated. *Should I cancel it? I will have to explain to the girls where I am going, and that might give rise to childish comments, young people being what they are.* "It might be better to wait until the case is closed."

"I'm sure it would," Griffiths replied. "But then I'd be back in London, and you'd be here in Norfolk. It's almost now or never, my love."

Mary was glad he couldn't see her blushing. *Ridiculous in a woman of my age.* "Ponsonby may not be back in time to drive me to the restaurant..."

"I'll send a police car for you."

"You'll do no such thing," Mary retorted. "I'll drive myself."

"Do you have a license?"

"I do. I just may be a little out of practice."

"Sneak out of the house when the girls aren't watching, and I'll pick you up." Griffiths chuckled, clearly understanding her difficulty.

Mary ground her teeth. "I'll tell the girls, and you be here at the house at eight, no later."

He laughed and agreed he'd be there on time.

Mary returned to the breakfast room and recounted her conversations with both policemen about the case.

"They'll be grateful enough for our help when they find we've solved their cases for them," Margie said, rather crossly.

"I'm sure they will," Mary soothed.

"Our theory explains who killed the man the skeleton belongs to and why he's buried here, who killed Zaclan and why, and who killed Quiggly Smythe and why. Really, it's so simple they must be kicking themselves." Winnie all but patted her own back. "I think we have enough."

Dotty cocked her head. "Simple isn't always right."

"What's wrong, Dotty?" Mary asked.

"Inspector Fletcher told us Mr. Smythe was with 'business associates' at the time of Zac's murder. If he can't break that alibi, then Smythe didn't kill Zac. Someone else did."

The others were quiet for a moment until Margie finally said, "Well, we've still explained two murders, the Smythe and the skeleton. If Lady Mary's neighbor didn't kill Zac, we just have more digging to do."

"Maybe Abernoothy will explain that when he's questioned," Winnie replied. "I think we have to wait for further developments to do more."

19

CLEARING THE WEEDS

Just as Mary had expected, breakfast the next morning quickly turned lively as the girls pressed her for every detail about her dinner with Griffiths. By the time it was over, she almost wished she'd never met with him. Only, she didn't, so she put up with the girls' silly banter and leading questions with as much grace as she could muster.

All that day, Mary waited for the phone to ring. She didn't know if she most wanted Fletcher to call and say Lord Abernoothy was innocent, though he had seemed the perfect suspect, with motive and opportunity, or he'd been arrested. Or if she wanted Griffiths to ring and say he'd enjoyed their evening together as much as she had. In the end, it was Griffiths who called, much later than she'd hoped for, but he made up for his tardiness by saying all she had wished him to say.

Fletcher, however, didn't call, even as the hours ticked away. No news came from the police as to Abernoothy's guilt or innocence. Mary kept busy with the daily affairs of the estate, and the girls tended to Barkley and a rowdy tennis match. Everyone was on edge waiting for news of what the inspector had uncovered about Abernoothy.

Late that evening, Mary was finishing up with her correspondence, when the telephone finally rang. Her heart raced as she waited for Ponsonby to make the announcement. "My lady." He nodded, holding out the handset.

When she got to the line, Fletcher's voice crackled, his tone brisk. "Your Grace, I apologize for the lateness of the call, but I wanted to inform you we've cleared Lord Abernoothy of any involvement in the murder of Mr. Smythe."

Mary took a step backward bumping into the wall. "Cleared him? But how can that be? I'm sure he had every reason to want Quiggly Smythe dead. What reason have you found to exonerate him?"

There was a pause, and Mary could almost hear the inspector weighing his words carefully. "I'm afraid I can't discuss the details. We've followed the evidence, and it leads us away from Abernoothy. He wasn't even in Norfolk at the time of the murder."

She tightened her grip on the phone. "Inspector, I'm not satisfied with that answer. You've asked me to trust your judgment, but you're giving me no reason to. What did you find that clears him?"

"I'm sorry, Duchess. There are aspects of this case that are... delicate. We're still pursuing every lead, but Abernoothy is not our man."

The line went dead. Mary placed the receiver back on its cradle, a frown creasing her brow. *What's the inspector hiding? Clearing Abernoothy without fully explaining it.* She huffed.

I have to inform the others. She sighed. *The girls already turned in. I'll have to wait until morning.*

STEPPING out into the bright morning sun, she made her way to the tennis courts where the girls were engaged in a lively game. The rhythmic sound of the ball being struck back and forth combined with youthful laughter set her mind at ease for a moment.

"Lady Mary!" Dotty called, waving her racket in greeting as Mary entered the court and approached the girls. A ball *whooshed* right past Dotty's head. "Come to join us? We could use an extra pair of hands."

Mary flinched for Dotty, who barely seemed to have noticed the ball, and forced a smile. "I'm afraid not, Dotty." *Not after that near miss; this game is menacing!* "I've just had a call from Fletcher."

Barkley grabbed the errant tennis ball in his mouth and followed the girls as they stopped playing and immediately gathered around their senior sleuth.

"What did he say?" Winnie asked, wiping sweat from her brow.

Dotty bounced animatedly. "Is the case solved?"

"I'm afraid, it's just the opposite. He feels he's cleared Abernoothy," Mary said, her voice betraying her frustration. "The inspector won't explain how, but he insists Abernoothy had nothing to do with the murder. He said Abernoothy wasn't in Norfolk county when the murder happened. We can look into that."

Barkley growled, and Margie echoed his sentiment, her auburn brows furrowed. "Cleared? But that makes little sense. He had motive and means, even if not opportunity!"

"I know," Mary replied, feeling the same frustration gnawing at her. "But there's something else. The inspector wouldn't give me any details. He was tight-lipped about the whole thing."

"Police procedure." Winnie shrugged. "You know how they can be with their secrets."

Scooping up the ball from Barkley, Dotty tossed it, but the dog stayed put at her side. "Trying to keep us out of the case."

"There must be something serious about Abernoothy they don't want us to know," Margie said, a conspiratorial glint in her eye.

"Obviously," Dotty mumbled under breath, and Mary grinned.

She glanced back toward the house. "Whatever the reason, we have to accept it." They began walking back. *For now.* "But it leaves us at a bit of a loss, doesn't it? If Abernoothy isn't our man, then who is?"

The girls exchanged uneasy glances and followed.

"We confirm Abernoothy's location at the time of the murder," Mary said, after a moment. "Fletcher may be happy with that evidence, but if we can show he wasn't where he said, then he's back as my chief suspect."

Winnie led the group into the house, and Barkley shot in front of her. "He wouldn't need to be here, though. Would he? A man as rich and connected as he is could find someone to carry out the actual killing. People at that level of society don't do their own dirty work, do they?"

"Abernoothy is your old friend, Lady Mary," Margie added. "Others among your old friends will be the best people to ask."

"My old friends will stop speaking to me if I continue interrogating them the way I've been doing, but you're right, Margie. This thread is mine to pull on." *The investigation keeps twisting at every turn, and the path forward is murkier than ever.*

Mary asked, "What angles haven't we considered?" She followed the girls through the glass French doors and into the drawing room.

Winnie sidestepped Barkley and threw herself into a nearby armchair, and smirking, said, "None, but maybe someone will make it easy on us and just confess."

A wry smile tugged at the corners of Mary's lips as she turned to face her phlegmatic sleuth. "If only it were that simple. When was the last time any of you checked in with your parents?"

Rolling her eyes, Margie slouched in her seat. "We're adults, Mary. We don't *need* to check in with our parents," she groaned, tossing her hands up in exasperation.

Peering at the young lady sternly, Mary raised a single brow. "I'm aware, but it doesn't hurt. They might be worried, especially with you all knee-deep in a case involving multiple murders."

"I talked to my mother this morning," Dotty cooed, a sweet smile lighting up her face as she adjusted the bracelet on her wrist.

Mary leaned over and patted Dotty's hand. "Thank you, dear. That was thoughtful of you."

"Not exactly," Dotty admitted. "I haven't been happy with the Abernoothy idea and wanted information from my parents. They claimed not to know anything."

"Your parents have never met Lord Abernoothy, dear. How would they know anything? They don't move in the same circles." Then, realizing this sounded like she was suggesting Dotty's parents weren't quite grand enough for Abernoothy, she clarified, "I mean, Abernoothy is ten years older than your father and lives in a different location of the country."

Dotty seemed to turn over some idea in her mind and was likely not listening to Mary at all.

Winnie shifted uncomfortably in her chair, her face fixed in a frown. "I still haven't phoned my mother or father," she admitted with a frown. "It's strange, though. They've been out of touch for days, which isn't like them."

Mary waved her hand dismissively, though a flicker of concern crossed her mind. "They're probably just wrapped up in their own lives."

Winnie sighed dramatically, her expression twisted in mock disgust. "You're not wrong. After all these years, they're like lovesick puppies!"

Dotty giggled at that, while Mary shook her head, amused but thoughtful.

Barkley grumbled, and then Dotty twirled her hand around, enticing the dog to play. He ignored her and curled up for a nap.

I know the answer must be closer than they and I realize, maybe even hiding in plain sight.

20

A CLUE IN DISGUISE

Dotty

Sometime later, Dotty, still deep in thought, rose to her feet and began pacing the sitting room, her tennis shoes squeaking on the hardwood floor as thoughts darted through her mind like moths around a flame. "If it wasn't Abernoothy . . ." she mused aloud, her voice trailing off. She paused mid-step, tapping a finger against her lips, eyes narrowing as if trying to see the invisible thread tying everything together. "Then it must've been someone else—someone we've overlooked. Maybe they were here that day, or perhaps they live close by."

She spun around so fast Barkley jumped from his slumber. Her gaze swept over the group, with sharp focus, and the dog swiveled his head mimicking her. "We've been circling the same suspects, but what if the real culprit is someone hiding just beyond our line of sight, in the shadows? It's time to cast the net wider—"

"What shadows?" Margie asked, her face wrinkled in confusion. "You're talking in riddles." Barkley huffed and laid his head back down on the flat, quilted dog bed.

"Not actual shadows," Dotty replied absently.

"Do you mean the SNUF Society?" Winnie asked.

Shaking her head, Dotty answered slowly, "Not just them." She whirled from one side of the room to the other.

Winnie threw her hands up. "Well, who then?"

Dotty struggled with her inner turmoil as she stopped moving and spoke plainly in answer. "Well, *our* parents, for one example."

"What?" Mary snapped in a shrill tone, and Barkley was quickly to his feet on high alert. He went to Mary's side, then she dropped a hand over the arm of the wingback chair to pat him.

"Look, I know my ideas are often a bit off the beaten track but this time..."

"A bit?" Margie snickered. She and Winnie appeared to be as incredulous as Mary sounded.

"I don't mean *just* them, of course," Dotty replied, finally sensing the severity of their alarm, which she'd expected but underestimated. "I'm just using them as an example of someone who was here or nearby and appears to have no link to the murders."

"And what link could they have?" Margie demanded, standing up. "My parents are the dullest, most respectable people who've ever lived and couldn't have a connection to this." Winnie urged her to sit back down.

With a slight scowl of outrage, Mary answered, "Yes, Dotty, please explain yourself."

"All our mothers assisted you in your detective exploits in the past, Lady Mary. You told us so yourself, and they've told us stories about your adventures."

"Yes, as being good people helping to right wrongs," Winnie

retorted, crossing her arms and looking unusually petulant. "Not murderers."

Dotty hovered over to the windows behind the loveseat the other two girls were sitting on and spoke with her back turned to the group. "We know the skeleton was of a young London man killed in the 1940s and buried here almost at once." When she turned around, she found Barkley by her side staring out the window as well. "He'd been among the shady side of London Society throughout the late 1930s, and we believe Lord Abernoothy adopted him informally, hoping to give him a better life . . . at least that's what we were told."

"So?" Margie called over her shoulder.

Dotty sighed. The two girls craned their necks to see her. *I really hoped they'd put on their thinking caps when I first spoke.* Dotty raised a hand, her fingers curled around nothing, acting as though she was writing on an invisible chalkboard. She spoke like a teacher might have spoken to her class. Barkley mimicked her movements and raised his paw. "So, what if during one of your sleuthing adventures, Lady Mary, perhaps"—She pretended to check off several imaginary names—"one of our parents could have had dealings with the dead man or Lord Abernoothy or Mr. Smythe?"

"But why should any of them kill one or more of these victims?" Mary asked, her tone soft.

"I don't know that they did," Dotty said. "I'm only showing you there may be suspects we've not yet considered." She mimed underlining the list in the air, setting down the fictitious chalk, then wiping her hands. "What I'm saying is, there are people we haven't looked into who also may have known all three victims and may have had a motive for the murders. Your neighbors on the other side, Lady Mary, the Youngs, for example. They're in their fifties now, I'd say, which means they also could have been in London during the time of Neland's death." Dotty flounced down into the only remaining empty chair in the sitting room, her tennis skirts twirling around momentarily until she settled. Barkley trotted over behind her and perched next to the leg of her chair like a teacher's assistant.

"Oh, the Youngs," Margie vocalized with clear relief. "Yes, of course, I see it now. You're right, Dotty, we must widen our search even further."

Winnie straightened as if she had come around to the idea as well and asked Mary, "Do you remember the Youngs, or the dead man from that time? Did you come into contact with your neighbors in any of your investigations with our mothers?" Winnie asked.

Mary, who appeared to be deep in thought, answered, "Pardon, I was tracing back the timeline's math to figure out if Dotty's idea had substance. I remember nothing particular. We knew of Quiggly Smythe, of course. He was always there in the shadows, as Dotty would say."

"Was he a criminal?" Winnie asked.

"Folks believed it to be so, and there were rumors, but he was at parties held by those on the edge of society, as were many others of his ilk. They had their claws in many people who should've known better but lived rakish lives as artists, actors, or writers."

Mary hashed out her ideas, and Barkley remained steadfast by the young hazel eyed sleuth's side.

"And the skeleton?" Margie asked.

Mary tilted her head thoughtfully, her white hair perfectly coiffed into a bun. "If he's who the police say he is, he probably lived that kind of rackety life too. It took me a long time to remember, because I didn't know him, only 'of' him. And I vaguely remembered him as being attached to our friend Abernoothy. Even now, I'm not sure I really remember him or if my mind has just conjured up connections from being told his name and about the timing of his death"

"Wait! Where does the skeleton's family live?" Winnie asked. "Do they live nearby?"

"I believe they lived in India or somewhere there about. I expect they returned to London when India became independent, but where they live now, I couldn't say."

Dotty patted Barkley's head, murmuring sweet sentiments to him.

Winnie crossed her arms, leaning forward. "I'm betting on the skeleton's family. They could be right here in Snodsbury or nearby, and, like we suspect of Abernoothy, waiting for their son's body to be found to confirm it was Smythe who killed him. I'll handle that part of the investigation."

Margie raised her chin slightly. "I'm sticking with the Youngs. They too may have been part of London Society back then, and Smythe has probably had his claws into them ever since. 'Rackety people' you said Lady Mary, but even good people get dragged into destructive behavior when they're young and foolish—or so I'm constantly being told. I think they took the opportunity to rid themselves of Smythe when a chance arose. Another murder among so many others. The perfect cover. I'm going to dig into their background."

Thoughtfully, Mary cocked her head again. "And I'll reach out to some of my old acquaintances and see what they know." She turned to Dotty, who was still quiet. "What will you do?"

"*My* parents often visited an old school friend of my father's close to here," she whispered. "That's where I'll begin."

"Your parents?" Margie cried, paused, then said, "We didn't realize you . . ."

Dotty nodded, her eyes narrowing, and lips pressed together in a tight line. "Yes, mine are included on the list as well."

"Oh, Dotty," Winnie moaned. "I'm so sorry I snapped at you.

It never occurred to me that you might be worried about your own parents."

"I'm sorry as well." Mary added her own apologies. "I see now why you were so hesitant to explain. There's nothing to worry about, you know. Your mother is as honest as they come."

Apparently sensing the tension resolved, Barkley trotted to his dog bed.

"She is," Dotty said, nodding with a sweet smile.

The silence that followed was heavy. The three sleuths headed upstairs to their rooms to change clothes and prepare for a day of investigation.

When back in her room, however, Dotty waited until she heard the others moving about in their own rooms, then she slipped back down the stairs, only stopping the moment she saw Mary and Ponsonby entering the drawing room. They didn't appear to see her, so she continued into the sublevel where she found Cook.

"Cook," Dotty chimed loudly, above the clatter of pans, to get the elder woman's attention. "I'd like to know who the chambermaids were that cleaned the rooms when we had the garden party's overnight guests here?"

She replied, grinning, "Good day to you, Miss Dotty."

"Sorry, hello," Dotty replied, not in the least put out. She and Cook were old sparring partners, though it was usually over Dotty's too frequent depredations of Cook's larder and pantry.

"The usual maids, miss, why?"

"Are they here today? Can I speak to them?" Dotty asked.

Cook fixed her cap. "You mean, will I fetch them?"

"Well, yes," Dotty replied. "They wouldn't listen to me."

"Does Her Grace know you plan to interrogate her maids, miss?" Cook asked, with one peculiarly bushy eyebrow quirked.

Shaking her head in an unusually serious gesture, Dotty answered, "She knows I'm investigating my parents while they were here and immediately after."

"She'll have to know."

"If I learn anything useful, she'll be the first I tell," Dotty replied, her eyes narrowed and lips pursed. Arguing with Cook was becoming worrisome. Someone might overhear and spread the word.

"Very well." Cook slung the hand towel over her shoulder. "You wait here, and I'll bring them to you." She hurried into a room beyond the kitchen and out of sight.

Cook re-entered a moment later with the two maids hot on her heels. Dotty stood in front of the pair—their tight expressions and crossed arms. It was clear they didn't like the idea of being questioned. A tense silence stretched between them, and the air felt thick with suspicion.

Dotty cleared her throat, adopting her most soothing smile. "I want to assure you, I'm not here on my own. The Duchess herself has asked me to gather some information. You're not in any trouble, I promise."

Shoulders of both maids dropped, and the tension in their faces softened. "All I wanted to know was if either of you noticed anything odd or unusual in those days of the garden party?" Dotty asked, when they seemed more relaxed.

They shook their heads in unison before one said, glancing at the other for confirmation, "The police asked that, and we told them we hadn't."

Noticing the phrasing, Dotty said, "Her Grace and I aren't the police. Did you maybe notice something you felt wasn't important?"

They glanced at each other for guidance, then the same girl

said, "A towel was missing, and then it was back. We thought nothing of it because guests often mislay towels, though I don't know how they do that."

"So when the police asked, you didn't mention the towel," Dotty said.

"Well, no," the now confirmed spokeswoman replied. "We'd have been in a right stew if we'd sent the police off on a wild goose chase. And her ladyship wouldn't have been pleased to have her guests embarrassed because they'd mislaid a towel. And we were right not to, for the next day, there it was in the laundry."

"Whose room was it missing from?" Dotty asked, trying to conceal her excitement.

"Couldn't say," the spokeswoman of the duo replied. "We only noticed when we'd gathered them all up."

This was disappointing, but Dotty still hoped for something. "When you say 'in the laundry,' was it muddy, as if it had been used outside, or dirty in some other way?"

"It weren't dirty at all, miss," one maid replied. "It was clean, though wet. I think they'd spilled something on it and washed it themselves so no one would know."

Was something washed off, and if so who did the washing? Where was it hidden when the police searched the grounds? Did they search the house?

Dotty leaned forward slightly, her hands clasped in her lap, her eyes fixed on the maid that had been answering her questions. "Did the police search the house the day of Smythe's murder?"

The maid fidgeted with the hem of her apron. "Not the day of the neighbor's murder, no. That was all outside, see?"

That caught Dotty's attention. She tilted her head, considering the implications. *Why didn't they search the house? Why was it immediately ruled out?*

She straightened, her curiosity growing. "And since the murder, after the police questioned you . . . has anything struck you as unusual?"

Again, they shook their heads in unison.

"No arguments? No raised voices?" Dotty pressed.

This time, one maid hesitated, biting her lip and shaking her head slowly.

Dotty narrowed her eyes. "What is it?"

"I don't like to say," the maid muttered, glancing nervously at her companion. "It weren't nothing, really. Well . . ." the maid began, her voice low and uncertain, "Mr. and Mrs. Winters were . . . very cross about something that day."

Dotty's expression softened. "Do you know what it was about?"

The maid shook her head again, quicker this time. "No, miss. They didn't argue in front of us."

Thoughts were swirling around in the sleuth's head. "And you don't know why they were arguing?" she asked, patiently.

The maid shook her head. "He said it didn't matter because he was dying, anyway. Leastways, that's what it sounded like to me. It was the only thing I heard clearly, but it makes little sense. He appeared as well as anyone."

Keeping the growing suspense in check, Dotty asked, "Are you sure that's what he said?"

"Not sure, like," the maid replied, suspiciously, "like I wouldn't swear to it. That's just what it sounded like."

"Okay, thank you. You've both helped me a lot."

After dismissing them, Dotty waited a sufficient amount of time before returning to the kitchen to advise Cook about what had transpired.

"Mind you tell Her Grace, Miss Dotty," Cook admonished. "No running off and doing something daft and landing yourself in trouble."

"You mean like the Duchess would've done when she was my age?" Dotty replied, then darted away avoiding any scolding from Cook. She scampered up the stairs to the ground floor where she was pleased to find no one in sight.

Dotty crept back to the door to the drawing room, where she could hear the duchess and Ponsonby in a low discussion that sounded very serious.

I mustn't interrupt. With a wide grin, she trotted lightly upstairs to change out of her tennis clothes and grab her coat, hat, and handbag, then quietly left Snodsbury by a side door to avoid being seen.

***

DOTTY WALKED to the village Post Office, greengrocer, and bakery, changing her pound notes and half-crowns into pennies —taking over the village's only phone box.

Fortunately, it wasn't in great demand on this summer's afternoon, and, with the helpful post office telephone book, she could track down and speak to her own parents, before talking to Margie's and Winnie's parents. With that done, she set off back to Snodsbury.

Parents! Margie's words kept echoing through Dotty's head... *parents were the most boring people in the world. It's what all children think and yet...*

Her mood was somber as she walked. Although she momentarily delighted in being right, unfortunately, her despair at what she had learned from the so-called boring parents overwhelmed that happiness, and her heart ached.

21

THE SNUFF OF SUSPICION

When Mary's three assistants left the drawing room to get ready for their investigations ahead, she rang the bell for Ponsonby to join her in the drawing room for a conference.

Ponsonby and Barkley were at her side once she'd settled into her favorite chair. "Yes, my lady?"

Picking up her needlepoint, she asked Ponsonby without preamble, "What can you remember of the days prior to the war?"

"A lot of parties and visits," Ponsonby stated. "I think everyone sensed another war coming, and most took the approach of savoring life while they could."

Mary sighed. "I agree. It was a frenetic time. I thought you might remember more of it than I do." She didn't need to mention that she and her husband were often deeply embroiled in the festivities of such parties that her mind had muddled the details. *My trusted butler and friend here knows that very well.*

"The specifics may be fresher in my mind, my lady, but I had only an observer's role and naturally an outsider's view of it."

Barkley plodded around in a circle and harrumphed as he

settled by the elegant Adam fireplace—eliciting a chuckle from Mary.

It's true. Ponsonby drove us to parties or the stately homes where we stayed for days indulging with champagne and enormous meals, but he could only see what the other staff saw.

"My neighbors, the Youngs, came up in a conversation today," Mary said. "I couldn't be sure if they were part of our crowd back then. He doesn't ring a bell, but she might have been there. She would have been still using her maiden name. Do you remember either of them?"

Ponsonby shook his head politely, saying, "I don't recall ever seeing her prior to returning to Snodsbury." Barkley snored softly.

"What about Abernoothy and his young friend?" Mary continued placing delicate stitches on a keenly priced handkerchief. "The one whose skeleton has been lying in my garden for nearly two decades?"

Grimacing, Ponsonby replied, "I remember Lord Abernoothy and the young person, my lady. A most unwholesome young man." She glanced away from her stitching and peered at him.

The butler cleared his throat and added, "As a matter of opinion, of course."

"No, no, I agree. Badly brought up, I suspect. Extremely rude to everyone, as memory serves me vaguely."

"Quite, my lady."

She resumed her stitching. "And what was your opinion of my fellow sleuths from that time?"

"Delightful women, though I'm sure their parents were unhappy with the adventures they were taking part in."

Mary agreed once more. "Much like the generation of girls we have with us now and their parents. I was more than once given a lecture about leading impressionable young women astray, I recall. Did you ever see them with the deceased, or with my neighbor, Quiggly, perhaps?"

"Ah, I see. No improprieties that I can recall ma'am," Ponsonby said. "I recall all the young ladies being fond of the young man though."

"He was very attractive," Mary replied and clipped her floss. "Much like our young gardener and three young sleuths now." *Funny how the past presents itself here in the present.* "Anything about Quiggly Smythe?" she asked as she placed her glasses onto the bridge of her nose and threaded a strand of a different color onto the brand new embroidery needle without problem.

"Nothing was amiss, however. There were long ago rumors among the staff involving Abernoothy, the man, Quiggly, and of course others of a similarly shady nature."

"Anything specific that you can remember that applies to this modern day case?"

"I'm afraid not, my lady, only snippets come to mind. If there was anything solid, regarding nefarious activities, I would've told the police when they asked."

Mary frowned, while expertly tying into her previous stitches. "It would've been helpful to have something concrete before phoning my friends from that time, something to jog their own memories."

He hesitated but finally asked, "What has brought on this line of enquiry, my lady?"

She set the stitching down, having no stomach at this time for the intricate work. "Dotty suggested that maybe one of my assistant sleuths from those long-ago days, the mothers of our sweet girls, may also have a motive for our present murders because of something that happened back then," Mary said. "At first I was skeptical, while my mind tried to conjure up the days.

I then became fearful that Dotty may be correct. And I can't think why. Something is there at the back of my mind, and I can't seem to bring it forward."

"When they look into those far-off days, Chief Inspector Griffiths and his men may consider us both as possible suspects, my lady. At the very least, reassure him you're not who he's looking for," Ponsonby suggested.

"Yes, yes, I know, but speaking to him about it may make him more suspicious rather than reassure him," Mary argued. "Let sleeping dogs lie, I say. What rumors did the staff share among themselves back then?"

"Just rumors, my lady. Just idle gossip, and not to be factual. When we told Inspector Fletcher that Abernoothy had always been sure it was Quiggly Smythe who had his young friend killed and buried, that reminded me of the rumors of the day. There were some who said they heard Smythe on the phone planning it."

"Seems unlikely," Mary replied. "Would he do anything so foolish as to plot like that in a stranger's house?"

Ponsonby's impassive expression twitched. "It was in his own London house, my lady, and it was his own staff that heard it."

"Then why did the police let Abernoothy go?" Mary cried. "It's as we said. He murdered Smythe."

"I'm sure they had their reasons," Ponsonby said, his tone flat.

Mary's suspicion flared. "What aren't you telling me, Ponsonby?"

"You might not be aware that Lord Abernoothy has an alibi for the time of the murder," he replied. "I've only just learned of it myself this morning."

"Through the Butlers' Club, I presume?" Mary asked.

With down turned lips, Ponsonby answered, "Quite so."

Mary realized this was something she could not get from her old friend. She'd have to ask other friends, and that could be part of her conversation when she phoned them.

"Is there nothing you can think of to help jog memories?" Mary asked Ponsonby, again. Everything Ponsonby had said was more or less confirmation of her own memories and those she'd spoken to before telling Chief Inspector Griffiths about Abernoothy's involvement with the skeleton as a young man, but there was nothing new.

Again, hesitation on Ponsonby's part made her aware there was something that was troubling him. *The Butlers' Code is as strong as any Freemason's Oath*, she thought.

Her butler spoke slowly, obviously choosing his words with care. "I remember there were scurrilous rumors that your neighbor did not murder the young man. It was suggested that Oliphant vanished due to matters involving a woman. Sadly, the woman's name was never mentioned, if she even existed. Your assistants from those days may remember that gossip. After all, they were of similar ages and went to the same entertainments."

"I don't," Mary said. "And I went to the same events."

But Ponsonby had taken up his wooden stance and expression, which she knew meant he was trying to spare her feelings.

"How would such a rumor start?" Mary asked, still hoping for more.

"I never gave it any credence then, and still don't. Only . . ." His gaze drifted ever so slightly.

Mary cocked her head. "Only what?"

Ponsonby's jaw tightened, a faint twitch at the corner of his mouth betraying his struggle to maintain his usual composed demeanor. "Only . . ." he paused, then relaxed. His mind made up. "Only at different times, I saw your assistants, and others, with the young man. Knowing the young man's behavior toward others, particularly to the servants, I disapproved, but it wasn't my place to speak, so I didn't. It was a relief to me when he disappeared."

"Then you think Dotty might have stumbled upon the truth?"

"I couldn't say, my lady. She may have simply suggested her mother and her friends' mothers as a line of inquiry by accident, or she may have, over the years, heard conversations she didn't understand then but now thinks she does."

"If what you and Dotty are suggesting is true," Mary said in horror, "then I've been criminally blind."

"We don't know any of this is true, my lady. And if it is, how were you to know? The young man was murdered in 1940, when London was being bombed every night, and hundreds were already dead or missing."

"You're right, of course," Mary replied. "Still, if it's true, I shall feel I failed." She smiled. "You've given me what I need, my old friend. A new thought to spur their memories. Thank you."

Barkley stirred to his feet and followed as Mary and Ponsonby left the drawing room together, her butler to return to his duties and Mary to begin, once again, interrogating her friends. She seated herself in the small hall cubicle set aside for the phone and closed the door. *These conversations might be more private than usual.*

Nearly an hour later—and likely much poorer once the phone bill arrived—Mary left the booth and returned to the drawing room. Her heart felt as if it had sunk into her stomach. Before sitting by the window to think, she rang the bell for Ponsonby.

He'd clearly been waiting for her call, for he arrived only a moment later. Mary asked for Darjeeling tea to be brought in for both of them. "We need to talk before the girls return," she told him.

When the maid had carried out domestic arrangements and

left the room, Mary began, "I think Dotty and your rumor were right."

Ponsonby didn't reply. He knew her well enough to know when she would need time before she could go on.

Taking a deep breath, and mentally giving herself a shake, Mary recounted what she'd learned and how she interpreted what she'd been told. It made for a sorry tale of betrayal, despair, and finally, deaths.

MARY FOUND it hard to wait for the return of her assistants. Even as they did, Dotty first, then Margie, and finally Winnie, she asked them to say nothing of their findings until the entire Society of Six was assembled, including Cook. From the expression on Dotty's ashen face, Mary understood the girl knew the truth as well.

When the young sleuths and Cook were all assembled, along with Barkley and Ponsonby, she began, "I have a lot to tell you from my own investigations today but, in case there's anything I've misunderstood from listening to my old crowd, I'd like to hear what you learned." Mary glanced around at their eager faces, all expecting to hear her thoughts. Cook removed her cap and sat.

"Margie, you could start us off. What did the Youngs have to say?"

Margie glanced around the group before saying, "Well, you already talked to Mrs. Young on the phone before I arrived, Lady Mary..."

"Yes, I did, dear. I thought it best they knew you were asking on my behalf."

Margie nodded. "She said that. Anyway, it did the trick. Mr.

Young is away on business, but Mrs. Young was more than willing to answer all my questions."

Winnie leaned in, raising a brow. "And those were?"

"I asked if she or Mr. Young had been in London Society in the years leading up to the war. She said no. They weren't part of the circles that would grant them access to such events, nor would they have wanted to be."

Dotty focused her eyes on Margie. "So you learned nothing?"

Margie shook her head, firm. "I didn't say that. They lived in London, met, and married there. While they weren't part of the high society crowd, they knew plenty about the lifestyle young people, like our parents, were living." Her eyes narrowed as she locked onto Mary. "She still reads gossip columns but also remembers rumors from her own social circle—stories about the lords, ladies, and the people we're investigating." Margie studied Mary's face.

Mary blushed. "I may not have been as explicit as I should have been in my description of what we were all doing back then. It isn't until these recent events that I've truly thought we were dangerously foolish."

Sighing heavily, Dotty asked, "But, did you learn anything useful, Margie?"

She shook a head full of unruly red curls. "Only hints and rumors. Nothing we can positively use as proof. She said they had heard of a murder, but she didn't know who or how."

"You were there all day, and that was what you got?" Winnie bemoaned.

Margie shifted uncomfortably. "I kept the conversation going as long as possible, hoping something she didn't understand might shed light on our inquiry. She seemed happy to have someone to talk to."

"Thank you, Margie," Mary said, before Winnie or Dotty

could chime in. "You did well. How about you Winnie, what did you learn?"

Winnie still appeared dismayed at Margie's lack of detail but nodded and said, "Had a devil of a job tracking them down, the skeleton's family, I mean."

"It's amazing that you managed at all," Mary said. "The war created so much confusion and chaos—his people could be anywhere."

"Kent, actually. Not too far away," Winnie continued. "They answered the phone, so I had a good long chat with his mother. I phoned from upstairs, though, I'm afraid the bill will land on your doorstep, Lady Mary."

Mary sighed. "I was on the phone for an hour myself," Mary replied, ruefully. "I think between us we may have bankrupted the estate. When did you phone?"

"Just hung up," Winnie replied.

"And what did you learn?" Mary smiled sadly.

Winnie shifted her weight, staring at the fire before continuing. "As you remembered, Lady Mary, they *were* in India when their son disappeared. They didn't return until after the war, so unfortunately, they know nothing that could help."

Mary leaned forward slightly. "No family in England at the time? Anyone who might have known something?"

"They had a daughter, but she was already married and living in Kenya when the war started. Actually, they wanted their son to join her in Kenya to avoid conscription," Winnie explained. "For a while, they prayed he'd gone into hiding."

"Unpatriotic, don't you think?" Margie muttered.

Winnie gave a small nod. "The mother noticed my disapproval and told me, 'You'll understand when you have children of your own.' And perhaps someday I will."

Mary raised a hand gently to steer the conversation back. "A mother's fears aside, was there anything else, Winnie?"

Winnie shook her head, a hint of frustration crossing her face.

Margie, not missing a beat, grumbled, "And you gave me grief over my day's investigation?"

Winnie shot back, her tone sharp, "I thought the Youngs were our next best suspects. Believe me, it's just as upsetting for me to have nothing to show for it as you."

This is the moment I was dreading. "Dotty, what did you learn?"

On the verge of tears, Dotty whispered, "Everything."

"So it was your parents?" Margie and Winnie exclaimed in unison.

Dotty didn't reply. She stared at Mary, whose steady smile gave her the courage to begin. "I wish I'd never thought of our parents, honestly, I do. I wish I'd never mentioned my suspicions to you all."

"Cut it out, Dotty," Margie cried. "What are you saying?"

Folding her arms, Dotty muttered, "I'm saying I learned something today I want to forget."

"Just tell us, dear," Mary urged. "Tell us what you learned and how the story was told to you. That way, we can come to the understanding you have without arguments or denials."

With a quick nod of her head, Dotty relayed the play-by-play of her talk with the maids, and from her phone conversations with her mother, and then Margie's mother, and then Winnie's mother, each revealing more of the events of the past, the day Zac died, and then the timing of Quiggly Smythe's death.

"But who took the towel and returned it washed?" Winnie asked.

Dotty bit her lip, and her eyes sparkled with tears. "Your mother, Winnie."

"No!" Winnie shouted. "That's not true. They're lying."

"I spoke to your mother, Winnie. It's true."

Winnie shook her head adamantly. "I don't believe it," she cried. "Why would they?"

Dotty took a deep breath and began, "She said it all began years before, in early 1940. Against her wishes, the young man was pressing his attention on her one evening, and your father, before he was your father, stepped in to stop it. There was a brief fight, and the young man died."

"How horrible," Margie said. "But I'm sure it was an accident. Winnie's dad didn't mean to kill him."

"It was, and what happened horrified them, though they knew it was wrong, they couldn't face the scandal, the court and the newspapers. Your father, Winnie, was on leave from his regiment and hid the body. It would be another missing person among the rubble of the bombed-out buildings."

"But they didn't hide the body in London," Winnie pointed out.

Nodding, Dotty continued, "They realized that, if his body was found, even among the rubble, there may be questions, and people would remember your mother and the young man were often seen together."

"If he was as involved in Society as people say," Margie objected, "why would Winnie's mother feel so sure the investigation would focus on her?"

With a grimace Dotty answered, "It seems Winnie's mother and the young man had been very close until the time she met Winnie's father. The young man, our skeleton, couldn't accept her throwing him over and pestered her whenever he could."

"Love is often unreasonable," Mary murmured to herself.

The others glanced at her before turning back to Dotty. "Just tell us, Dotty," Winnie cried. "Dragging it out like this is torture."

Dotty was indignant. "I'm trying to, but you all keep interrupting!"

When there was silence, she continued, "Anyway, Winnie's

mum and dad remembered that Mary and her husband never visited Snodsbury anymore and decided that would be a safe place to bury the body. They drove out of the city after dark. Many people who had cars drove out of the city and slept in them to be safe from the bombs. They kept going until they reached Snodsbury where they buried the young man."

Winnie stared at Dotty as though she had lost her mind, her mouth opening and closing silently, as if trying to form words that refused to come. Her eyes glazed over, distant, from the weight of the revelations.

In tears, Dotty continued, "They didn't know what they would uncover when they attended the garden party. It was all so long ago. But when Zac led the garden tour and spoke of extending the grounds for his new rose bed, pointing to the very spot where he planned to dig, your mother panicked. They couldn't risk him finding the burial."

Still grappling with the puzzle, Mary said, "No one would have connected them to a body after all this time. Why would they be so concerned?"

Dotty wiped her eyes. "Winnie, both of your parents worked on the grave back then, and the next day your mother realized her bracelet was missing. They searched everywhere but never found it. She was sure it had fallen into the grave during the chaos."

"They feared the police would find it and trace it back to her?" Margie asked, her voice tight with disbelief.

"Yes. It was a family heirloom, engraved with her name and her mother's. They were terrified," Dotty whispered. "Your mother wanted to wait, but your father . . . He couldn't risk it. Zac's discovery would expose them. They framed Quiggly Smythe to cover their tracks."

"How could they do something so horrible?" Margie muttered, shaking her head.

"Your parents weren't thinking clearly," Dotty explained. "When the police cleared Smythe, your father was afraid they would still find that bracelet, pointing to him and your mother, Winnie. He panicked when Smythe called him, demanding a meeting."

Winnie's eyes flickered back to life, a frown tightening her features. "He thought Smythe was going to blackmail them? But how could Smythe know?"

Dotty nodded gravely. "You're right. He guessed Smythe must have stumbled upon the bracelet sometime, not long after it was lost, and finally understood what it was doing there in the garden and who it belonged to. Anyway, they met, and your father killed Smythe with an old walking stick from the hall. A heavy, antique piece—Regency, or maybe Victorian. Your parents cleaned it thoroughly afterward, wiping it down with a towel."

"That's nonsense!" Winnie's voice, usually composed, cracked with disbelief. Her pacing grew frantic, her hands twisting together, the emotional storm within her finally bursting free. "I *know* this isn't true. My father wouldn't do such things!" She ignored everyone's stares, her face flushed with anguish, before abruptly bolting for the door. Barkley followed in her wake, only to be left behind when she slammed the door shut behind her.

Margie moved to follow, but Mary raised a hand. "Give her some time. She needs to process this." She hesitated, then slowly sank back into her chair, tension hanging thick in the air.

Ponsonby cleared his throat softly, stepping forward. "It seems we've only heard Mrs. Winters' account of events," he said. "Miss Winnie might be unduly upset."

Dotty shook her head, her face streaked with tears. "I questioned it myself. But when I spoke to her mother, she brought her father to the phone. He confirmed everything. Right now, he's at the police station, confessing to all three murders."

"And the bracelet?" Margie asked, hardly wanting to hear the answer.

Dotty nodded. "Smythe had it. Winnie's father took it and Winnie's mother has it again."

22

BLOOMS AND BETRAYALS

Winnie

Winnie sat on the bed, shaking uncontrollably. Wild thoughts ran through her mind, all ugly and many violent. None of this could be true. She knew her father better than she knew anyone, and it was impossible that he could murder one person, let alone three.

How long she sat there, she couldn't tell. She barely noticed when Mary entered the room and sat next to her. Only when she felt Mary's hand squeeze her own did she realize someone was near. Winnie swiveled her head slowly, and her eyes met Mary's.

"He couldn't," Winnie said.

"You're in shock," Mary murmured. "Try to relax. There's hot sweet tea on the way. You'll feel better."

They sat together for another age before Mary handed her a mug. Winnie chortled. "A mug? At Snodsbury?"

"You need more than a teacup full, Winnie," Mary replied. "Needs must, you know."

Winnie sipped the warm liquid, and as the time wore on, she slowly felt better. "It was a real shock."

"Yes indeed," Mary responded. "Rest now, and we'll talk later."

"No. There's something wrong, but I can't put my finger on it."

"What do you think it's about?" Mary prodded.

Rubbing her temples, Winnie closed her eyes. "I don't know, my mind's a muddle, but something still isn't right."

"Answers often come to us in our sleep," Mary said optimistically. "There've been many times I went to bed mulling over a problem and woken the next morning with the solution."

Winnie placed her finger on her chin. "If I just think clearly for a few minutes, I'll have it."

"Very well," Mary said. "Lie down, close your eyes, and go over everything you know about this story. I'll wait here with you."

"I'm no child. Please, don't coddle me."

They sat together as the room darkened.

WINNIE'S EYES SNAPPED OPEN, her heart pounding as the early morning light filtered through the curtains. In the quiet stillness she had reconciled, the truth clear to her now. The details were worse than the story she'd heard yesterday. But there was some solace in clarity. *For now, I'm satisfied. That will have to be enough, because I'm not happy. I may never be happy again.*

A light knock on the door, abruptly interrupting her ruminations, was followed by the soft creak of the wood. Mary entered the room, her usual grace clear in the way she moved, though there was a slight tension in her posture.

"Good morning, Winnie," Mary greeted, her voice gentle but

probing, as if sensing the storm brewing behind Winnie's composed expression.

Winnie barely glanced at her. "I know," she whispered, the weight of her realization hanging in the air like a thick fog.

Mary blinked. "What do you know?"

"I know my father couldn't have murdered Zaclan," Winnie replied, her tone steady.

There was a brief silence. "How do you know?" Mary asked.

"That afternoon," she began, gaining strength as she spoke, "my father said he wasn't feeling well. He needed to lie down. I remember being so worried about him. You know how strong he's always been, how rarely he ever takes to bed. It was unlike him."

Mary nodded slowly, the lines of worry on her face deepening. "And?"

"My concern grew until I couldn't stand it. I left everyone, only for a few minutes, and went to my parents' room."

"I knocked quietly on the door, and when he didn't answer, I was frightened, and I went in. He was asleep. Deeply asleep. There was a bottle of pills by his bedside. I was even more frightened and went to him. He was sound asleep. I read the pill bottle. They were to be taken daily, but the bottle was full so he hadn't taken an overdose or anything like that. I thought about the long journey, the heat, and the fact he's been complaining of tiredness lately. I decided it just meant he was growing old and needed an afternoon nap. I left him asleep."

"You don't think he could have been pretending or was asleep but woke the moment you left?" Mary asked.

She shook her head. "No. I'm sure he couldn't have. There is something wrong with what my mother said."

Mary responded, "Dotty spoke to your father as well. He came to the phone and confirmed what your mother said."

Winnie scowled. "She did it. He's protecting her."

"Think of what you're saying, Winnie. Your mother murdered three grown men, and your father will go to the gallows to save her?"

"Yes!" Knowing it sounded absurd, she quickly thought through an answer that would explain herself better. She'd always thought of herself as 'daddy's girl' and not her mother's. Was she just being contrary because of it?

"But how, Winnie?"

Frowning, because she still hadn't gotten the events clear in her mind, Winnie began, "Zaclan was drugged and easy to kill, so a woman could have done it."

"But Mr. Smythe?" Mary asked.

"Hit on the back of the head by something heavy, a walking stick like a cudgel you said. Well, a woman could swing a walking stick as easily as a man, and its weight would have done the rest," Winnie said, becoming excited as she saw her way to an explanation that made sense.

"A young man years ago?" Mary reminded her.

"Maybe there was a struggle," Winnie replied. "Maybe he fell and hit his head."

"He wasn't killed by a blow to the head, though," Mary replied.

Rudely, Winnie replied, "I didn't say he was. He may have been unconscious, and she finished him in a way that left no damage to his bones." She hesitated, then cried, "Or, he pounced on her, and she was holding something like a knife, a letter-opener maybe, and she accidentally stabbed him."

"If it was an accident, why would they hide the body?" Mary asked. "After all, a woman defending herself would have the sympathy of the court, especially with that man's reputation."

With the case solidified in her mind now, she spoke calmly. "I don't know. Perhaps there was some reason it didn't look accidental. Perhaps there was some circumstance in their relationship that would lead a jury to think it wasn't an accident? We can't know. Only my parents really know, and I'm going to get the truth out of them."

Mary nodded, which to Winnie looked like sympathy and not agreement.

Winnie threw her hands on her hips. "I will get the rest of the story out of them."

"We need to be clever to do that," Mary replied. "If your father really is protecting your mother, just walking up to him and asking will only get a flat denial."

"He loves me," Winnie said. "If I tell him I can't live without him, he'll see his way to telling the truth."

Mary's expression changed, and Winnie asked, "What?"

"Dotty said the maids had heard him say something like *he was dying anyway*," Mary replied. "Your ploy won't work because I suspect he knows you're going to lose him, anyway. At least, his way, you get to keep one parent. Your way, you lose both."

"Mother was your fellow sleuth back then," Winnie said. "How do you suggest we get them to tell the truth?"

Mary frowned. "Winnie, do you really want to lose both parents? Your father dead from some fatal disease, and mother possibly hanged?"

The seriousness of Mary's tone prompted Winnie to pause. She'd been so caught up in saving her father, she hadn't seen that getting him back meant losing her mother. To go on meant choosing between them. She saw now why her father was doing what he was doing. It was for her, and she should respect his wishes and the gift he was handing her.

"Take some time to think it over, Winnie," Mary urged her. "It's what your father would want, or he wouldn't be doing it."

After a moment, Winnie said, "Zaclan was killed horribly. However nasty your nosey neighbor was, he appears to be innocent of either of the two murders and didn't deserve to die like that. I know nothing about the skeleton's death, but the two deaths I do know about are enough for me."

Sighing, Mary replied, "If you're right, and it is your mother who is the murderer, then I agree with you, but for you, this will always be a nightmare. Your actions may lead to your mother's demise, and you'll always remember it."

Winnie nodded unhappily. "I understand. It's odd, I've never thought a lot about good or bad, right or wrong, and if asked, I would probably have said I cared little. Yet, here I am choosing the path of justice to the peril of my mother's life."

"What will you do?" Mary asked.

"I'll visit my father today and explain to him that my evidence will clear him of killing Zaclan, and, in doing so, cast doubt on the other two murders," Winnie replied.

"It may not change his mind," Mary said. "After all, the prosecution will say you're a loving daughter trying to save her father and your evidence isn't true."

Winnie shrugged. "Then I'll tell Inspector Fletcher what I know, and he can search for more evidence. They still have the area roped off, I suspect they won't find footprints that match my father in there, now that they know what they're looking for."

"And that walking stick may have traces of your mother on it, rather than your father." Mary leaned forward "The police didn't have a murder weapon. Now they do. The truth may come out naturally, you know."

"If my father said that's what they used, they made certain his fingerprints were on it and not hers."

Mary nodded her agreement. She'd thought that too.

"And," Winnie cried, her sad expression vanishing as she said this. She was now overjoyed. "Fletcher can examine my mother's sleeping pills. I bet that's what she used to knock out Zac."

"Get dressed, my dear," Mary said, her voice heavy with

sorrow as she rested a hand on the girl's shoulder. "Ponsonby and I will take you to the police station after breakfast."

"I couldn't eat breakfast." Winnie shook her head. Her eyes wide, brimming with unshed tears. Her shoulders slumped as if the weight of the world rested upon them.

Mary offered a sad smile. "You should, you know. This will be a long day."

MARY'S PREDICTION PROVED ACCURATE; it took a considerable wait before Inspector Fletcher could meet with Winnie to take her statement. According to Fletcher, the forensic experts then returned to Snodsbury in search of evidence to support Winnie's account, and contact was made with Chief Inspector Griffiths in London to investigate whether any proof existed of an affair between the young man and Winnie's mother leading up to his death. Winnie remained at the station to "assist the police with their inquiries," while Mary and Ponsonby headed back to Snodsbury.

It was lunchtime before Fletcher would let Winnie visit with her father, and the result was exactly as Mary had predicted. He told Winnie on no account must she challenge the statement he'd made confessing to all three deaths.

"Father," Winnie told him, when it was clear he wouldn't budge from his sacrifice. "I know why you're doing this. You want to save me pain, and I thank you for that. But your death in this way will give me more pain than anything you can imagine. I love and admire you. I won't let you die in a way that shames you and your memory."

"Your memory of me won't be spoiled, Winnie," he said, his

eyes glistening. "Believe me, this is for the best, both for you and me."

Moments after the exchange, two officers led her father from the room, leaving Winnie alone, lost in quiet contemplation. There was something she didn't yet know, and her father was shielding her from it. *What could be worse than knowing my mother is a murderer?*

Winnie paced back to the waiting area, her nerves raw while she waited to be collected by Ponsonby in the car, but the minutes dragged on. Each tick of the clock churned up new, unsettling theories, her mind racing through his motives, each worse than the last.

Mary's Rolls-Royce arrived, and Winnie was ushered into the rear of the car. She sank into the leather, as the door clicked shut behind her.

As the car glided through the streets, and into the open countryside, Winnie's composure broke. Tears welled up, spilling down her cheeks as she stared blankly out the window. The weight in her chest grew unbearable, and no matter how hard she tried, she couldn't push away the creeping horror that twisted her thoughts, threatening to consume her. She realized at last what could be worse than knowing her mother was a murderer. *My father is not my father! My real father is the skeleton found under the roses. My father, stepfather I should call him now, married my mother because he loved her and couldn't bear to see her ostracized by Society.* She let this run through her mind, desperately trying to prove it wrong, but every objection only made it more real.

Worse, when she stopped denying it, she found it answered so many other questions. For instance, the reason they hadn't owned up to the young man's death was because no one would believe her mother hadn't killed him in anger when he refused to acknowledge his future child. It also explained why she'd seen her stepfather always more loving to his wife than her mother was to her stepfather. Something she'd always noticed but had put down to the difference in their characters, hers cool and calculating, his affectionate.

The car stopped outside the entrance to Snodsbury, and Ponsonby opened the passenger door for Winnie to step out. Winnie, however, was unwilling to leave its shelter. With the door open, and Mary, Dotty, and Margie waiting, she had to. Their expressions of deep pain did nothing to ease Winnie's own feelings.

"I want to be alone," she said, walking past them before running up the stairs to her room.

23

THORNS BENEATH THE ROSES

Mary

The next day Mary called for Winnie to join the group. Winnie's footsteps were slow and hesitant as she finally descended the stairs, crossed the hall and entered the sitting room.

"Come in, dear," Mary said, meeting her at the door and guiding Winnie to a seat. "Do you feel up to telling us what you know?"

"I have a lot to tell you all. None of it is proof, but I know it's true."

"Everyone here is your friend, Winnie," Mary told her. "What is it you want to say?"

In a stronger voice than Mary had expected, Winnie recounted what she knew and what she'd realized when her father had still refused to change his story. She also told them his explanation for why he refused to do that.

"But Winnie," Margie said, hesitantly, "your mother could

never have overcome Zac and held him down. No matter how certain you are, that's a fact you can't explain."

"You don't know any of this for certain, Winnie," Margie said, her hands fidgeting with the edge of her sleeve, as her eyes darted nervously between Winnie and the floor. "There's still a possibility of a different explanation."

Winnie shook her head. "I know it's true. Father and I have always been close, and I know this is the only thing that would persuade him to commit suicide, for that's what this is."

"Then you must tell him you know, Winnie," Mary said. "And let him know that whatever the circumstances of your birth, he is now and always has been your father. That may be enough to stop him from going through with this charade. You may even get months longer with him than you will if he follows his chosen path."

"I intend to tell Chief Inspector Griffiths," Winnie said, nodding her head. "If you'll phone him for me, Lady Mary. He might find the proof I need, and he needs to close his case."

"Inspector Fletcher should know too."

"Yes, I'll speak to him after," Winnie said. "I need the inspector's permission to speak to my father again. I think this time, when I tell him what I now believe to be the truth, he'll see there's nothing more to be gained. Then the police will find evidence to confirm my theory, and he'll have to spend his last days being nursed by me."

"Maybe I should speak to your mother, Winnie," Mary said. "When she knows what you believe to be true, she may wish to change her story, if she hasn't been telling the truth."

"No, Lady Mary," Winnie said. "She's gone this far to escape justice. We can't know how much further she might go."

Margie intervened. "But maybe that would be for the best, Winnie. If your mother lives abroad, beyond the law's reach, and your father is shown to be innocent and released, then you'd have both of them with you for as long as they live."

Winnie shook her head. "This isn't about me anymore. It's about right and wrong and the consequences of each. I thought a lot about it overnight, you see."

"I'll phone Chief Inspector Griffiths," Mary said. Her heart was heavy, but it was yet another opportunity to talk to Ivor whom she missed more with each passing day.

"Thank you," Winnie said. "The sooner I've told him, the sooner I can persuade Inspector Fletcher to let me speak to father again."

By mid-morning, Mary and Winnie were once again at the police station, waiting for the promised interview.

"Remember, he's agreed to let me speak to your father after you do," Mary said. "If you find you can't sway your father, come away, and let me try. He and I have known each other for decades now. That might count for something."

"I remember," Winnie said. "But if telling him I know he isn't my biological father doesn't work, I don't know what will."

Settling down for a long wait, Mary sighed as they escorted Winnie into the interview room where her father would be waiting.

I can't imagine what might be going through Winnie's mind at this moment.

The clock ticked slowly, but Winnie came back too quickly. Her porcelain skin was blotchy and wet with tears. "I was right. He didn't want me to know he wasn't my real father. Not my 'real father' is what he said. I almost stomped my foot, and I really wanted to smack him."

"Will he drop this terrible charade now?" Mary asked.

Nodding, Winnie's curtain of black hair jostled. "He's making a new statement to Inspector Fletcher right now. If he tells the truth this time, Fletcher says, they will arrest and charge my mother today. I'm to tell no one." She paused, before saying, "And nor must you, Lady Mary, after all she's one of your oldest friends."

Mary's brows furrowed. "Did he say what happened to the young man?"

"Yes," Winnie replied. "Mother confronted him about her condition, and he was dismissive and unpleasant. The argument became a struggle, and as I guessed, he was accidentally killed. At least, that's what my mother told my soon-to-be stepfather when she asked for his help."

"He must've been, and I suppose still is, hopelessly in love with her to do what he did," Mary mused quietly.

With a grimace, Winnie added, "He thinks everything would've been perfect, if you hadn't rebuilt your gardens. He'd said, 'If only you'd done that next year, none of this would have happened.'"

"I see his point, but I refuse to share the blame because I did some gardening," Mary retorted.

A smile played on Winnie's lips. "He wasn't apportioning blame, only commenting on how the timing led to his involvement in the two recent deaths."

"Has he any involvement?"

Winnie shook her head. "In Zaclan's no, at least, only in not reporting what he learned was the truth. But, in your neighbor's murder, he helped clean the cudgel and placed his fingerprints on it to deflect blame."

"And how was it that Zac couldn't defend himself?" Mary asked.

"My mother takes Chloral Hydrate to help her sleep," Winnie replied. "The moment she saw where the rose beds were, and heard Zac's plans to extend them, she knew she had to act. She put enough of her medicine in a drink and cajoled Zac into drinking it. She can be quite pushy when she needs to be. When she saw him go out again to see why or who sprayed us, she followed him knowing he would soon black out."

Rising, Mary nodded. "We should return home." She crossed the floor to the Desk Sergeant and asked to leave a note for Inspector Fletcher. With the note written and handed over, she and Winnie left the building.

However, as she stepped off the last of the front steps, Mary saw Inspector Fletcher heading toward them.

"A sad business," he said, when he reached them.

Mary nodded, hardly able to speak.

"I wanted to thank you for all the information you and the young ladies provided," Fletcher said. "Without it, there would be no good outcome in this case."

"Thank you, Inspector," she replied. "It will mean a lot for the girls to know that the police appreciated them in helping to solve the case."

"Yes," Fletcher said. "Well, I thought you all should know. I may have been hasty at the outset, and I wouldn't want you to think my opinion hadn't changed."

Mary laughed. "A 'bit hasty' is right." She would have said more, but Winnie's expression standing silently at her side, stopped her. "Everything about this case has been painful to us all. We'll say no more about it."

"What will we tell the others?" Winnie said, as the Rolls hummed through the country lanes back to Snodsbury.

"The truth as we know it," Mary replied. "And we'll ensure no one phones out from the house until Inspector Fletcher phones to confirm the arrest."

"You think Dotty and Margie's parents might call my mother?" Winnie asked.

"We have all been friends since school," Mary said, sadly. "They may have feelings of loyalty that go beyond what justice demands. It's safest if they don't find themselves in a position where they must choose."

Winnie nodded, silent as the hedgerows slipped by the window.

Mary understood Winnie's silence. Inspector Fletcher had told the girl that if her father made a full and honest statement, he'd be released on bail and could return home. Winnie had said she'd nurse him through his last days, but Winnie was no nurse. She must be wondering what she could do to help.

ONCE AGAIN GATHERED in the drawing room, the group listened quietly to Winnie recounting the morning and its outcome.

When Winnie finished, Mary said, "I asked Inspector Fletcher to phone me once they completed the police procedures. We must not, on any account, talk about this until we hear from him."

Nods of understanding swept through the assembly. This ending certainly caught them all off guard, and unmistakable pain etched across many faces.

When Ponsonby answered the phone, it was mid-afternoon, and the assistants were already outside on the terrace. He made Mary aware that it was Inspector Fletcher.

"Bring the girls, Ponsonby," Mary told him, taking the handset. "Inspector, what news do you have?"

He briefly told her. Winnie's mother was in custody and charged with two murders. Winnie's father would be bailed tomorrow, if she and Winnie wished, they could collect him from the station when the formalities were complete.

"Did she say anything?" Mary asked.

"I'm not at liberty to say what the accused has said, Your Grace, as I'm sure you know," Fletcher replied formally. "I *can* say she is maintaining her right to silence, and her lawyer is with her now."

"The moment Mr. Winters is to be released, please have someone phone me, Inspector, and we will collect him," Mary told him, as she saw Ponsonby and her assistants entering the drawing room. "Thank you for letting me know what's happening." She put down the phone and joined the others.

"So, it's over," Winnie said, dully, when Mary finished speaking.

"Our part in it is," Mary replied, nodding. "It's up to the police and the courts now."

"Will you take Mr. Winters straight home tomorrow, Lady Mary?" Margie asked.

"I thought maybe he might want to spend a day or so here where the police can come and interview him further," Mary said. "But I'm sure he will want to go home as soon as possible. What do you think, Winnie?"

Winnie nodded, her lip trembling.

The phone rang out in the hall, and Ponsonby went quickly to answer it. Returning a moment later, saying, "It's Chief Inspector Griffiths, my lady."

Mary left the room almost as quickly as Ponsonby had. "Yes, Ivor," she said, picking up the handset.

After brief greetings, Griffiths said, "We followed your marriages and births suggestion, and, yes, Winnie was born less than six months after her parents married. It's not impossible that she's his, but they had no more children, which is perhaps suggestive. We can never know for sure."

Mary's face softened, her shoulders sagging slightly. "Poor Winnie," she said, her voice low. "To have your entire world broken like this in the space of a week must be devastating."

"I'm sure you and the others will help her through it," Griffiths said. "None of this reflects badly on her, after all."

"Will she see it that way, though?" Mary responded.

"Only time will tell," Griffiths replied. "I feel we have enough now to close out the case of the unfortunate young man in your rose bed. If I may be so bold, I'd like to join you at Snodsbury if not tomorrow, maybe the next day?"

"Yes, it would be nice to get together," Mary said, blushing at her prim response.

"I'll phone when I'm free."

24

THE BLOOMING TRUTH

two months later

Mary stared out through the terrace door windows at the steady rain and the mist swirling across the lawn and gardens. *Summer is gone.* The sound of a door opening made her turn away from the view to see Ponsonby entering the room.

"Good morning, Ponsonby," she said. "I trust our guests are all still snug in their beds."

"They are, my lady," Ponsonby replied. "Apart from you, only the staff are up."

Mary nodded. "After all that's happened, I couldn't sleep. The sound of the rain pattering on my bedroom window was calling me to start the day."

"You must be excited to have the Chief Inspector for another visit," Ponsonby replied, with the hint of a smile on his face and in his voice.

"Yes, I am," Mary agreed. "Though I'd wished for better

weather. I feel autumn is upon us already. Our summers are so short, and I hate to see them slip away."

"We will have some nicer days during his stay, my lady. It's not October yet."

"I'm sure you're right," Mary replied, moving away from the gloomy scene outside the window. "Today, our guests will have to amuse themselves inside."

Her guests were Dotty and Margie and their parents, with the addition of Chief Inspector Griffiths arriving on a mid-morning train. Winnie and her father had stayed only one day before returning to their home.

"Was there something you wanted, my lady?" Ponsonby asked, gently reminding her she'd rang the bell for him.

Mary chortled. "If I did, I have forgotten what it was. I think it may have just been for company." She smiled at him. "I'd watched the rain so long, I'd grown melancholy, and I knew I could trust my dear friend, Ponsonby, to brighten my mood."

He smiled, uncharacteristically showing teeth. "It's kind of you to say so. After the excitement of the summer, I, too, feel low. The anti-climax after our success has been greater this time than with any of the other cases."

Mary nodded. "I feel that too. Whatever happens between Ivor and me will not affect you, Cook, or any of the staff here, you know. I, or we, if that's the future, will need all our old friends around us."

"Thank you, my lady," Ponsonby said. "However, if things should change, you need not feel any alarm on my account. The past few years have caused me to reflect on the possibility of retirement."

She spoke earnestly, her voice soft but sincere. "I hope you won't abandon us. If you wish to go, I won't stand in the way, but I'd love for you to stay."

"I would never leave Your Grace's service if I'm needed. I've only ever wanted what is best for you," confided Ponsonby, blushing faintly.

"Then we'll talk no more of retirement," Mary replied. "Snodsbury wouldn't be the same without you and Cook. It's your home as much as mine, and we'll all go on comfortably together—and we'll retire together. Only not yet." She beamed. "Is everything ready for the Chief Inspector's arrival?"

"It is, my lady," Ponsonby replied. "And the car is being brought around as we speak. Will Your Grace be joining us on the drive to the station?"

Mary considered. "It's not accepted practice for a duchess to greet her guests at the station," she said. "But this is almost 1960 and a new world. Yes, I will go to the station and start a new fashion."

"Whatever Your Grace does is always fashionable. How could it be otherwise?" He hedged a wink.

25

A SHIFT IN THE GARDEN

another five months later

Mary, along with Ponsonby, Cook, Dotty, Margie, and Winnie—the Society of Six, an unlikely group of amateur sleuths born from a silly joke—gathered in black finery in the Winters' drawing room after Mr. Winters' funeral. Despite the unseasonably warm February weather, the chill in the air cut through Mary's bones, and she and the girls huddled near the fireplace for warmth.

"What will you do now, Winnie?" Mary asked, watching as the young woman gazed distractedly into the dancing flames.

Winnie startled, as if pulled from deep thought. "I'll sell the house and deal with the family affairs before deciding, I suppose."

"You know you'd be very welcome to stay with us at Snodsbury," Mary said, glancing at Ponsonby and Cook who both nodded.

"Or with us," Margie said. "Dotty and I are looking to rent a flat in London soon." She wrinkled her nose and continued, "We must find work of some kind."

Dotty peered past them and said, "The three of us could start our own detective agency."

Winnie made a sad attempt at a smile then shrugged, her shiny black hair neatly trimmed to rest at her shoulders. "Maybe. I'll know better when I've settled things."

Mary didn't dare mention the sensational trial now being broadcast on every news outlet in the country. She wondered if they should discuss it. Somehow, not mentioning it made it seem more obvious than speaking of it.

"When might that be?" Mary asked.

"Soon," Winnie replied, absentmindedly, for she was once again staring into the flames as if seeing her future in them. "Soon."

"You must keep us informed," Margie said. "We want to help in any way we can."

"Of course," Winnie said, suddenly drawing her attention away from the fire. "You must excuse me; I see people preparing to leave." She hurried away to thank neighbors who were on the point of going.

"We mustn't let her brood," Dotty said, quietly. "Or be too long alone."

Mary and Margie nodded, and Mary said, "I agree. This quietness doesn't bode well. I fear the daily news is preying on her mind, and her conscience is troubling her."

"It can't be anything but troubling," Mrs. Marmalade agreed, speaking for the first time since they'd arrived back from the church. "To know you were instrumental in your mother's eventual . . ." she paused, ". . . punishment is a terrible burden to bear."

"We should get back, my dear," Mr. Marmalade suggested.

Dotty's parents gestured in agreement, and the older members of the group took their leave of Winnie.

"We're staying to help Winnie clear up," Margie told Mary, who was also preparing to go. "Will we see you soon?"

"Next case that comes my way, you'll have a call from me," Mary replied. "And I hope the reverse is true."

"If our detective agency gets a really juicy case, you can be sure of it," Dotty told her.

With that, Mary departed, leaving her three assistant sleuths to their own devices.

SEVERAL WEEKS LATER, as Mary and Ivor read the morning paper over breakfast, a thought came into Mary's head. She'd resolutely stopped her mind from endlessly going over the investigation, helped by the making of arrangements for her private marriage to Ivor Griffiths. But now that was over, and it seemed her mind still had unanswered questions about the case.

"Ivor," she said, sharply, for he had become absorbed in the news and might not hear her. "Did your police doctor ever tell you if Margie's theory would work?"

As she'd expected, he looked puzzled at the question.

"You remember," she said. "About lacing snuff with heroin and selling it that way."

"Oh, that. Yes he did, but like all experts too late to be helpful for the investigation."

He seemed about to return to his reading so Mary said, "And?"

"He didn't think there could be enough heroin in each pinch of snuff to make it a lucrative outlet. I think that's probably true."

"You didn't think to tell me?"

"They wrapped up the case, my dear," her new husband replied. "There was no need."

"I would have liked to know, and I'm sure Margie would too," Mary snapped.

"Sorry, I've been busy lately with that docklands murder. It slipped my mind."

Ponsonby entered the room. "The morning post," he announced, presenting first Mary and then Ivor with the tray on which the letters lay.

Mary glimpsed a postcard of New York City's skyline, which she picked up and turned over.

'Dear Lady Mary,' it read. 'I've taken a trip. Home is just too ghastly right now. 'Till we meet again, all my love, Winnie.'

She glanced at Ivor who'd already guessed. "Winnie has gone abroad?" Already back to reviewing the remaining mail, Mary nodded.

"I can't blame her, poor child," he replied. "I would too, in her shoes."

"Do you think she'll return?" Mary asked, but Ivor's attention was already back to the newspaper, and she didn't get an answer. *I know in my heart she won't come back, but I hope she finds peace and happiness in the States.* Mary peered out the window at the work of the new gardener. *Let's hope he finds nothing else buried out there!*

Did you know? Reader reviews are very important to an indie author's success? They validate our work and help others find our stories. If you enjoyed Royally Snuffed please leave a happy review filled with stars.
Amazon.com/review/create-review?&asin=B0CLGPMPV6

As an added thank you, here's a free gift! Click here to tell me where to send it ~ Kathryn
https://dl.bookfunnel.com/vozzqxufnv

If you jumped in here at the end you can circle back to the start by reading Royally Dispatched, *the first book in this trilogy.*

Leave a review!

Thank you for reading our book!
We appreciate your feedback and love to hear about how you enjoyed it!

Please leave a positive review letting us know what you thought.

THANK YOU! × × ×

ABOUT THE AUTHOR P.C. JAMES

P.C. James, Author of the Miss Riddell Series
Author Bio: P.C. James is the author of the quietly humorous Miss Riddell Cozy Mysteries, the One Man and His Dog Cozy Mysteries, and co-author of the Royal Duchess and Sassy Senior Sleuths cozy mysteries.

He lives near Toronto in Canada with his wife, and they have two grown children and now a grandson.

He loves photographing wildlife in the outdoors yet chooses to spend hours every day indoors writing stories, which he also loves. One day, he'll find a way to do them both together.

You can find his books on Amazon here:
Miss Riddell Cozy Mysteries
https://www.amazon.com/dp/B08MQXFRK7

One Man and His Dog Mysteries
https://www.amazon.com/dp/B0CG3ZCJ3V

Amazon Author Page
https://www.amazon.com/stores/author/B08VTN7Z8Y

And more from the author here:
Facebook:
https://www.facebook.com/PCJamesAuthor

Bookbub:
https://www.bookbub.com/authors/p-c-james

GoodReads:
https://www.goodreads.com/author/show/20856827.P_C_James

His Newsletter Signup Here:
https://landing.mailerlite.com/webforms/landing/x7a9e4

ABOUT THE AUTHOR KATHRYN MYKEL

Kathryn Mykel, author of Best-Selling Quilting Cozy Mysteries

Inspired by the laugh-out-loud and fanciful aspects of cozies, Kathryn Mykel aims to write lighthearted, humorous cozies that play on her passion for the craft of quilting. Kathryn is an avid quilter who resides in New England with her dog Bentley.

Website:
www.authorkathrynmykel.com

Facebook
https://www.facebook.com/AuthorKathrynMykel

Bookbub
https://www.bookbub.com/profile/kathryn-mykel

GoodReads
https://www.goodreads.com/author/show/21921434.Kathryn_Mykel

Award-winning author of best-selling quilting cozy mystery series:
Sewing Suspicion
2021 Indie Cozy Mystery Book of The Year
Quilting Calamity
2022 Indie Cozy Mystery Book of The Year

Quilting Cozy Mystery Series:

Sewing Suspicion (Book 1)
Quilting Calamity (Book 2)
Pressing Matters (Book 3)
Mutterly Mistaken
(Holiday Pet Sleuths Series) (Book 3.5)
Threading Trouble (Book 4)
Paw-in-Law
(Holiday Pet Sleuths Series) (Book 4.5)
Stitching Concerns (Book 5)
Purrfect Perpetrator
(Holiday Pet Sleuths Series) (Book 5.5)
Mending Mischief (Book 6)
Doggone Disaster
(Holiday Pet Sleuths Series) (Book 6.5)
Patchwork Perils (Book 7)
Seaming Uncertainty (Book 8)
~ **Coming Soon** ~
Beach Brawl (the book inside the books)
Whipstitching Worries (Book 9)
Needling Nemesis (Book 10)

Stand-alone Books:
I Pittie the Yule (Christmas Novella)
Dead End (Halloween Novella)
Fine Points Are Sketchy (Quilting Cozy Mystery)
A Load of Trouble

- Sassy Senior Sleuths
- Sassy Senior Sleuths Return
- Sassy Senior Sleuth on the Trail

Travel can be murder. Can Miss Riddell and Nona catch the villains before they become victims?

Miss Pauline Riddell befriends a strangely lovable, fly by the seat of her pants amateur sleuth, named Gretta Galia aka Nona. The two sixty-five year-old travel companions visit tourist traps around the United States.

These stories move forward about twenty years from the Miss Riddell Series by P.C. James and back in time about twenty years from the Quilting Cozy Mystery series by Kathryn Mykel. Approximating the setting of these stories to be during the turn of the 21st century, between 2000-2005.

Made in the USA
Middletown, DE
18 January 2025